SLAPPY, BEWARE!

GOOSEBUMPS®

Also available as ebooks

ALSO AVAILABLE:

Goosebumps

SLAPPY, BEWARE!

R.L. STINE

SCHOLASTIC INC.

To Jane Stine, Joan Waricha, and Susan Lurie,
the brains behind the screams

INTRODUCTION

R.L. STINE HERE, EVERYONE.

Readers, beware—you're in for some *special* scares!

I don't usually get to introduce my books and say hi to you. But, as you can probably tell, this book is a little different.

Yes, it's a hardcover book. And you will find illustrations inside, for the first time ever.

That's because this is a special collectors' edition. This book marks the **30th Anniversary of Goosebumps**.

THIRTY YEARS of ghosts and ghouls, screams and howls, twists and surprises. There are more than 150 Goosebumps books so far. How many have *you* read?

Of course, we couldn't have this **Celebration of Scares** without one character—Slappy, the evil dummy.

How did Slappy come to be alive? I'll tell that story in this book.

Why is Slappy so evil? I'll explain that, too.

And I'll also tell you about the *worst* day in the evil

dummy's life. Yes, the day that could be Slappy's *last day alive on earth*!

The end of Slappy forever? Can you stand it?

I won't keep you in suspense any longer. Let's start the story . . .

PART ONE

200 YEARS AGO

Where did Slappy come from? What brought him to life?

There are many stories and legends about Slappy's origin.

Some say that an evil magician carved him out of wood from a haunted coffin. One story goes that he escaped from a puppet factory in Cincinnati. Another legend says that the ghost of a ten-year-old boy lives inside Slappy's head.

I'm not sure about those stories. I think the story I'm about to tell you is the true one.

Slappy's story starts two hundred years ago in a tiny village in Europe. So let's head there—to a cottage at the edge of the deep woods. That's where you will meet Darkwell the puppet-maker. He is also a sorcerer.

Darkwell is going to cast a secret spell. A spell

that will change many lives as it travels through the centuries.

What is this mysterious spell, you might ask?

What is this curse that's been kept secret for two hundred years?

Be patient, readers. Let me tell you the story . . .

Flames crackled in the fireplace. They sent shadows leaping and dancing over the walls of the small cottage. Outside, the wind moaned, shaking the glass in the windows and whistling through the cracks in the thin walls.

Feeling a chill, Ephraim Darkwell pulled his gray robe tighter around him. The old man's hood fell over his forehead, covering his long white hair. He leaned over his workbench, his hand moving a knife quickly, smoothly.

Darkwell's deep gray eyes locked on the rounded piece of wood he was sculpting. A head. He rubbed his thumb over its scalp, brushing away a splinter. He worked the slender wooden eyelids up and down.

The face was nearly completed. Darkwell knew he had little time to finish. He had heard the rumors. The talk in the village. He had explained to everyone that he was a simple doll maker, a builder of puppets.

But the superstitious villagers didn't believe him.

They spied on him. From the woods behind the cottage, they watched him through the cottage's windows. Somehow, they had learned the truth.

Darkwell was no simple puppet-maker. He was a sorcerer who could magically bring his puppets to life. A master of the dark arts. But he had vowed never to use his power for evil.

He came to the village to work in peace. To be left alone to build his creations and explore the magic he had learned. He meant the villagers no harm . . .

Until yesterday . . . when Darius Koben, the chief constable, burst into the cottage, grim-faced and wheezing in anger. That moment, Darkwell knew his peace had ended.

"You and your nephew must leave," Koben boomed, banging his cane against the floor with each word. "You are not wanted here. Your evil magic has frightened everyone."

Darkwell bowed his head. "I am a simple doll maker," he said.

Koben smacked the cane hard against the wooden wall. His cheeks reddened above his gray beard.

"Your lies cannot protect you, Darkwell!" he shouted. "You have been seen talking to your dolls—and they have been seen talking back. They move about your cottage as if they are alive. You cannot deny the truth. It is too late!"

"I mean no harm," Darkwell insisted.

"I did not come to argue," the constable said, waving his cane in the air. "I came to warn you."

"Warn me?"

"There is talk in the village," Koben said, lowering his voice. "Talk of burning you out. The torches are already lit, Darkwell. Do you understand? The townspeople's anger—it cannot be controlled."

Darkwell stared at the constable, allowing his words to sink in.

"Get out!" Koben shouted. "Leave now! You and your nephew. Pack up and get out if you value your lives!"

The constable spun on his cane and stomped from the cottage. The slender door banged in the swirling wind. Darkwell pulled the door closed, feeling the cold air on his face.

He shivered, but not from the cold. He shivered in anger that his work would be interrupted. He was about to finish his most magical creation yet. He couldn't allow the foolish, ignorant villagers to destroy his masterpiece.

Darkwell leaned over the workbench all night, his hands working feverishly. And now he held the doll in front of him.

"Those fools will be sorry," he told the doll. "They have pushed me too far. Once you are finished, we will make them sorry they are alive."

The lifeless eyes gazed up at him. The wooden lips turned up in a grin. The head lay tilted to one side.

"Almost complete, my little friend," Darkwell said. But then he uttered a startled gasp as the cottage door swung open.

A figure staggered in. His hair flew wildly about his face. His white shirt was stained, one sleeve nearly ripped off. A trickle of blood ran from his nose. His cheek was cut, dark blood forming a crooked line.

"Isaac!" Darkwell cried, staring in horror at his twelve-year-old nephew. "Isaac! Isaac! What have they done to you?"

"Th-they beat me, Uncle," the boy stammered.

Darkwell swept his arms around him and guided him to a wooden chair. He brought a wet cloth from the pot beside the hearth and dabbed at the blood on his nephew's face.

"Who did this, Isaac?" Darkwell demanded. "Tell me the whole story."

"I . . . I went to buy the supplies you wanted," the boy began slowly. He smoothed down the sides of his coppery hair with both hands. "But they stopped me outside the village store."

"Who?" Darkwell asked gently. "*Who* stopped you?"

"They said you weren't fit to raise me," Isaac said, ignoring the question. "They said they could not leave me with someone so evil. They—they are going to take me, Uncle. Take me away from you."

Darkwell placed a hand on his nephew's trembling

shoulder. "I won't let them," he murmured in the boy's ear. "You do not need to worry."

"I . . . I tried to tell them you were good. I said you were kind. I said you wouldn't harm anyone. That's when . . ."

Isaac's words caught in his throat.

"That's when they beat you?" Darkwell demanded.

Isaac nodded. "I stuck up for you, and it made them angry. I tried to get away. But some boys grabbed me. They said their fathers were coming for us—with torches. Coming to burn us out."

"Don't worry, my boy." Darkwell patted his nephew's head. "You do not have any reason to fear. I will make sure of it."

He helped Isaac to his feet and led him to his cot against the wall. "Lie down. Sleep now. Sleep, and dream of good things."

Isaac obediently lowered himself to the cot and curled onto his side. "Good night, Uncle."

Darkwell stood watch until his nephew fell asleep. Then, shaking his head, he strode back to the workbench. He lifted the doll he had been crafting and brushed some wood chips off its chest.

"Your time has come," he said. He reached for the clothing he had sewn for the doll. He pulled the trousers over the legs, then worked the arms into the shirt and then the jacket.

"You will not disappoint me," Darkwell told it. "I have completed you just in time. When the villagers arrive to destroy me, you will be ready."

The doll stared back at him with glassy eyes. Its grin was frozen on its face. It sat hunched over on the worktable.

Darkwell propped it up so that its back leaned straight against the wall. He raised the head so that its eyes looked into his eyes.

"Yes! Yes! My heart is pounding!" Darkwell declared. "I have learned much magic and accomplished many things. But it has all been leading up to *you*!"

The sorcerer took a step back from the worktable. He cleared his throat loudly. His eyes on the doll, he took a deep breath—and shouted these words to the ceiling:

"*Karru Marri Odonna Loma Molonu Karrano!*"

3

Darkwell's hands trembled as he gazed at the doll. He tucked them under his robe and held his breath. The words he had just spoken rang in his ears.

The only sounds in the cottage were the crackling of the fire and the soft breathing of Isaac, asleep on his cot.

Darkwell stood frozen in place, waiting. Waiting for the magic to take hold. And then it happened. The doll's eyes blinked. They blinked once. Twice. The mouth closed slowly with a soft *click*.

"Yes," the sorcerer whispered. "Yes. It is working. You are alive." The old man took a deep breath and forced his heart to stop racing in his chest.

The doll blinked once more and turned its wooden head from side to side, as if testing it. The painted lips moved up and down, making a soft *click* each time.

"Speak!" the sorcerer commanded. "Can you speak?"

The doll raised a wooden hand and touched the side of its face. It blinked a few more times, moving its head up and down. And then a soft, harsh voice rattled from somewhere inside it: "Where am I?"

Darkwell cried out. "Yes! Yes! You speak!"

"Where am I?" the doll repeated. And then, in the same raspy voice, only stronger this time: "Who are you? Who am *I*?"

The old sorcerer hugged himself as if to hold in his excitement. "We have no time for questions," he told the doll. "They are coming to destroy me. But you are here now. You were created to carry out my evil when I am gone."

The doll blinked. Its mouth dropped open. "Evil? I'm evil? Tell me . . . why am I evil?"

"You are my revenge," Darkwell replied. "My revenge upon those fools who do not understand how brilliant I am . . . the fools who would destroy me. If they succeed, I am about to perish—"

"Perish?" the doll repeated.

"But my evil will live on through you," Darkwell continued. "I have cast a powerful spell. I have spoken powerful words to bring you to life. Listen to me carefully. I won't have time to explain it again."

The dummy lowered its hands to the workbench and leaned toward the sorcerer. "I am listening."

"From now on," Darkwell said, "when the secret words are spoken, you will awaken and perform the evil you were created for."

"What does that mean?" the doll demanded. "What should I do?"

"You will terrify people," Darkwell replied. "You will scare them to death. You will make people scream in fright and cry. And you will make them your servants for life."

"For life," the doll repeated.

"I have given you a cute name," the sorcerer said. "So that people will not suspect your true nature. Your name is Slappy. A name fit for a circus clown. But you are no clown. Instead of bringing laughter into the world, you will bring screams of horror."

"Hahahaha!" Slappy tilted back his head and uttered a shrill laugh. "Screams of horror. Father, that sounds like fun!"

Darkwell started to speak, but stopped. He heard voices in the distance. Through the small front window, he saw yellow lights flickering against the black night sky.

Torchlight? Were the villagers approaching?

Darkwell fought back the feeling of panic in his chest. "There is more I need to tell you, Slappy," he said, his eyes on the window. "I must give you a warning."

Slappy blinked. "A warning, Father?"

The sorcerer nodded. "The spell I have cast gives you great mind control powers. But beware of its one weakness."

10

Behind Darkwell, Isaac stirred in his cot. Eyes still closed, he stretched his hands above his head. "Is it morning, Uncle?" he called.

Darkwell ignored him. "Here is my warning, Slappy. You must do something evil *every day* that you are awake. If you are awake for a day and fail to terrify someone, the spell will end—and you will sleep forever!"

"Hahaha!" The doll let out its cold laugh once again. "This sounds like interesting work," he rasped. "I will obey you, Father. I will be evil every day that I am awake."

"You have no choice, Slappy," Darkwell replied. "If you fail to scare someone every day, you will sleep forever. *And no words will be able to wake you!*"

"Uncle?" Isaac sat up on his cot.

At the same moment, a sharp *thud* at the cottage door made the boy cry out.

Another hard *thud*. The sound of an axe chopping at the wood.

Darkwell grabbed Slappy in both hands and pressed him against the front of his robe. "The villagers!" he exclaimed. "They have come for us!"

Bright yellow torchlight flared outside the cottage window. Angry shouts nearly drowned out the *thuds* of the chopping axes.

Isaac ran to Darkwell and tugged at the old sorcerer's robe. "Help, Uncle! What shall we do? You promised—"

"I promised you would not have to worry about them," Darkwell said. He hugged Slappy to his chest, his dark eyes wide, fixed on the door. "I keep my promises, Isaac."

A deafening crash followed the *crack* of splintering wood. The door crumbled as it fell open. Heavy boots stomped over it as men in dark clothing and black hoods burst into the cottage.

Torch flames licked at the low ceiling. The voices of the men were loud and angry.

Darkwell slid Slappy to a corner of the workbench. Then he turned to face the intruders.

Chief Constable Koben pushed his way to the front, swinging his cane to scatter the men from his path. His face burned red in the bright torchlight. He raised the cane and pointed it at Darkwell. "You did not heed my warning, old man!" he boomed.

Behind him, the hooded villagers shouted angry words and jabbed their torches menacingly toward the sorcerer and his nephew. Isaac clung to his uncle's robe. Whimpers escaped his throat.

"You have no reason to invade my home and threaten me," Darkwell said, shouting over the murmurs of the men. He placed his hands on Isaac's shoulders. "I am a simple doll maker."

"We did not come for a discussion," Koben shouted. "We know what you are, and we will not have you in our village. We are decent people, and we obey the laws of nature—not the laws of darkness!"

"Burn the house! Burn the house!" some men began to chant. "Burn it down! Burn it all!"

Koben raised his cane to silence them. "Darkwell, we have come to put an end to your evil!" he boomed.

"Burn it down! Burn it down!" The flames appeared to grow brighter as the men stabbed their torches toward the ceiling.

Koben struck his cane against the floor. "Silence! We will burn it down—and this old sorcerer with it. But first we must deal with the boy."

"Noooo!" Isaac wailed. He held on tightly to the front of Darkwell's robe.

Koben took a few heavy steps across the room. "We want the boy," he said. "Hand him over to us. Your days are over, Darkwell. Your doom comes today. But the boy will be saved. We are taking him from you."

"Uncle, please—" Isaac whined. "You promised!"

Koben stretched out both hands. "Hand him over, Darkwell. Hand him over *now*!"

A stillness fell as Darkwell stared back at the chief constable with his icy gray eyes. After a long moment, the old sorcerer broke the silence.

"As you wish," he said. "Here he is. You can take him."

"Nooooo!" Isaac wailed.

Darkwell grabbed the boy's wrists and pushed him toward the chief constable. "He is all yours," Darkwell said.

Koben blinked in surprise. He seized Isaac around the waist.

Isaac cried out again—and struggled free. He dove back to Darkwell and clung to the front of the sorcerer's robe. "Noooo! Please—! Noooo!"

The hooded men looked on in stunned silence. Their low murmurs stopped. The torches in their hands locked in place.

"The boy is yours," Darkwell said again. He shoved Isaac toward Koben.

Koben gripped Isaac again. He started to pull him to the door.

"Wait," Darkwell said. "Please. May I have a moment to say good-bye to him?"

Darkwell reached under his robe. He pulled out a

large metal key. He stepped up to Isaac and swept up the back of the boy's thick hair.

Koben's eyes went wide as Darkwell pushed the key into the back of Isaac's head. Everyone heard a sharp *click* as the sorcerer turned the key.

Isaac's eyes closed. His mouth fell open. His knees collapsed. He dropped to the floor.

Koben shouted in horror as Isaac's head hit the floor and cracked open like a walnut. Gasps rose throughout the cottage as everyone stared at the wires and tubes inside the head.

Darkwell tucked the key under his robe. "I promised Isaac he wouldn't have to worry about you," he said.

Koben took a few staggering steps back until he bumped into the startled men. "The boy—he . . . he isn't real!" Koben stammered, pointing his cane at the body on the floor. "He is one of your creations!"

A thin smile crossed Darkwell's face. "One of my best," he said.

"Burn him! Burn him *now*!" a man shouted.

And the others took up the chant. "Burn him! Burn him! Burn him!"

Swinging their torches, they stormed forward. Darkwell raised both hands as if to shield himself.

The ceiling caught fire. A chair and Isaac's cot burst into flames. Then, with a crackling explosion, the workbench began to burn.

Coughing and choking in the thick black smoke, the hooded villagers turned and ran. Constable Koben bent to pick up the broken Isaac doll. But then he changed his mind and he, too, tumbled out the door.

Darkwell shielded himself from the smoke and fire with the front of his robe. The workbench sizzled and burned behind him. He swept Slappy into his hands and, clutching him to his chest, ran into the night.

Constable Koben and the hooded villagers watched at the edge of the woods. Many had dropped their torches inside the burning cottage, but a few still flamed in their hands.

"You will not escape, Darkwell!" Koben's voice echoed in the shadowy trees. "You have committed crimes against nature. Tonight, we will make sure you pay for those crimes!"

"Burn him! Burn him!" the hooded men picked up their chant again.

Two men, their torches pointed, moved toward the old sorcerer. The orange flames sputtered in the wind, then trailed behind them like fiery snakes.

Darkwell called out in surrender. He took a few steps back as the men advanced.

Then everything seemed to freeze as the doll sat up in the sorcerer's arms. Slappy's eyes went wide and his hands flew up at his sides.

"ENOUGH!"

His scream made several villagers gasp. One of them dropped his torch, and the tall grass smothered the flames.

"ENOUGH!" Slappy's cry rang through the woods.

The hooded men huddled closer together. No one moved.

Koben raised his cane. "More evidence of your crimes, sorcerer!" he shouted. "This talking demon proves that your evil magic must be ended tonight!"

The villagers gasped as Slappy tossed his head back and laughed. "Hahahaha!" A shrill, cold laugh. "Thank you all for the drama and entertainment!" the doll cried. "But Father and I will be leaving now!"

"You will leave in flames!" Koben shouted. He signaled with his cane for the men to attack with their torches.

But they stared in shock as Slappy raised both

hands above his head and shouted a stream of strange words . . .

"Lambda Osiris Karamunder Dominus Malado Venn!"

The ground shook. Tree branches cracked. The villagers uttered choked gasps. And froze where they stood. Even under their hoods, their fear could be seen.

It was as if time had stopped. None of the hooded men could blink or breathe or move. They stood as still as statues. Even the flames in the torches froze and hung stiffly in the air.

"We can go now, Father!" Slappy cried, his shrill voice ringing loudly in the frozen silence.

But Darkwell held back. His eyes remained on Koben. He squinted hard into the man's bearded face—and saw Koben blink.

"Your spell has not worked on the constable," Darkwell murmured.

Koben let out a furious growl and came charging at Darkwell, the tip of his cane pointed at the sorcerer's belly. "Your evil cannot work on the righteous!" he boomed.

"You may want to rethink that," Slappy called out. He swung both hands above his head once more—and Koben stopped, inches away.

"Have a good trip!" Slappy shouted.

He swung his hands higher—and Koben took flight, his boots sailing up from the ground. The cane fell from the constable's hands as he floated into the night.

His hands grabbed at the air. His feet kicked frantically as he soared higher, above the burning cottage . . . above the dark, still trees. His scream faded as he flew into the distance. Then out of sight.

Silence returned to the woods.

Darkwell raised his creation in front of him. "I have succeeded with you!" he exclaimed. "Your powers are wonderful!"

He took one last look at the ashes of his cottage. Then he tucked the grinning doll under his robe and took off, running into the forest.

"You will make history!" Darkwell declared. *"Evil* history!"

"Couldn't have done it without you!" Slappy exclaimed. "Hahahaha!" His cold laughter rang off the trees.

PART TWO
TAMPA, FLORIDA

CHRISTMASTIME, THIS YEAR

Well, readers, talk about a change of scenery! Let me move the story up two hundred years to today. And let's get out of that cold, angry village.

Here we are at Tampa Bay Middle School on a warm Florida day in December. You're going to meet twelve-year-old Reggie Foreman, standing backstage in the school's big auditorium.

Does Reggie have any idea that he and his sister are about to enter a World of Pain?

Of course not!

Reggie is watching his ten-year-old sister, Poppy, from the side of the stage. Poppy is in front of the curtains, perched on a tall wooden stool, strumming away on her banjo. A yellow spotlight shines down on her, so bright Reggie can see the drops of sweat on her forehead.

It's the Holiday Talent Show, the last day of school before winter break. Reggie is ready to perform next. He has his dummy, Junior, tucked under one arm. He feels excited, not nervous.

Reggie knows his ventriloquist act is funny. With his large round eyes and goofy smile, Junior is always a big hit with the audience.

Reggie is worried about Poppy, though.

She has made a few mistakes during her banjo solo.

But Reggie should be worried about other things.

What *exactly* should Reggie be worried about?

And what does this have to do with Darkwell, our sorcerer?

Be patient, readers. You know I'm going to reveal the answers . . .

Reggie watched his younger sister, Poppy, onstage and shuddered.

Did the kids in the auditorium notice her mistakes?

Reggie hoped not. Poppy wanted to impress her friends.

And then . . . *ping*.

Reggie watched a banjo string break.

He heard Poppy gasp. She stopped for a second. Then she picked up playing.

She's being brave, Reggie thought. But under the bright spotlight, he could see the tears in her eyes.

"Bummer," Reggie muttered to himself. He knew that Poppy had spent weeks practicing her number. She even wrote an original holiday song for the show.

Reggie felt bad. His sister was using his old banjo. They should have put new strings on it before she started playing it.

But it's Poppy's own fault, he told himself. *She is*

always *copying me. Whatever I do, she wants to do, too. She should have picked a different instrument. But, oh no—since I played banjo in fifth grade, she has to play banjo, too.*

He could see the broken string waving in the air as she tried to strum. Poppy finished her song, jumped down from the stool, and took a small bow. The kids gave her some quiet applause.

Wiping the tears from her cheeks, she stomped offstage.

"Hey, Poppy, you were awesome!" Reggie called to her.

But she shoved him out of her way and kept walking.

Whoa, Reggie thought. *It's not MY fault. Maybe I can convince Mom and Dad to buy her a new banjo for Christmas. And I could give her some lessons. Poppy might like that.*

Onstage, Miss Harrison, the middle school principal, leaned over the microphone. "And now," she announced, "let's welcome Reggie Foreman and his funny friend, Junior!"

"Are you ready?" Reggie asked Junior. "Let's do this!"

Reggie raised the dummy in both hands and strode out into the spotlight.

Reggie dropped down on the stool and sat the dummy on his lap. "This is Junior," he told the audience. "Hey, why do they call you Junior?"

He pulled the string in the dummy's back and made the mouth open and close. "Cuz that's my name!" Reggie made Junior's voice gruff and deep.

"Well, Junior," Reggie continued, "how are you feeling today?"

"I'd feel a lot better if you didn't have your hand stuck in my back!"

That got a good laugh from the kids in the audience.

"That's not nice, Junior. I think you should say you're sorry," Reggie said.

"Hey, don't put words in my mouth!" Junior exclaimed.

"If I don't put words in your mouth, it will be pretty quiet up here!" Reggie said.

The audience laughed hard at that one. Some kids even clapped.

"Well, who's working *your* head?" Junior demanded.

More laughter.

"At least my head isn't made of wood!" Reggie said.

He made Junior's eyes blink. "*Your* head? I've seen better heads on a lettuce! I've seen a head of *cabbage* with more personality than you, Reggie!"

Big laughs.

"It's almost Christmastime, Junior," Reggie told the dummy. "What do you want for Christmas this year?"

"I thought maybe you could give me five thousand dollars so I can buy a cup of coffee!" Junior answered.

"Whoa!" Reggie replied. "Why do you need five thousand dollars for a cup of coffee?"

"I want to drink it in Brazil!" Junior answered.

More laughs and applause.

Reggie saw his friend Diego in the front row. Diego had already heard the whole act. But he was laughing harder than anyone.

Reggie felt good. The kids were laughing and clapping at every joke.

Now came the part that audiences always loved.

Reggie had a glass of water on the stage beside the stool.

"I want to show you a magic trick," Junior said.

"You know a magic trick?"

He made Junior nod his head. "I'm an awesome magician. I'm going to show you a great trick, Reggie. Pick up the glass."

Reggie reached down for the glass. "You want me to pick up this glass? It's full of water."

"Yes," Junior said. "Now lift the glass high and pour it over your head."

"Huh? You want me to pour all the water on my head? Give me a break, Junior. What kind of trick is that?"

"You'll see," Junior said. "It's such an awesome trick. Pour the water on your head, and you won't get wet."

Reggie raised the glass over his head. "You're sure? I *won't* get wet? That's the trick?"

Junior nodded. "Go ahead. That's the trick."

"Well, okay," Reggie said. "Here goes." He slowly tilted the glass, and the water splashed down over his head, soaking his hair and his shirt.

"I knew it!" Junior cried. "That trick *never* works!"

Shaking water off his hair, Reggie stood up and took a bow. Kids cheered and clapped and stomped their feet.

Miss Harrison was still laughing as she stepped to the center of the stage. "We have a winner!" she declared. "Actually, *two* winners of our Holiday Talent Show—Reggie Foreman and Junior!"

More applause.

"Enjoy your vacations, people!" the principal said. "See you in January."

The auditorium lights came on, and everyone hurried out. Diego was waiting in the hall. He bumped knuckles with Reggie. "You were awesome! That was a riot!"

Reggie started to reply to his friend, but kids crowded in around him. They all wanted to congratulate Reggie and tell him how funny he was.

Reggie was eager to change out of his wet clothes. But he loved being the center of attention. And he loved that his performance had been such a big hit.

"Can I hold Junior for a minute?" asked Phoebe Miller, a girl in his class.

She didn't wait for an answer. She tugged Junior from Reggie's hands and bounced the dummy in front of her. "Hey, he's pretty heavy."

"His head weighs a lot," Reggie told her.

"Let me hold him," another girl said. Reggie felt helpless as kids passed the dummy around.

He raised his eyes from the crowd of kids around him and saw his sister watching from down the hall. Poppy carried her banjo case stiffly at her side. She had a glum scowl on her face as she stared at her brother.

She's giving me the evil eye, Reggie thought. *This means trouble.*

"Christmas is totally weird down here," Reggie's mom said. She passed the salad bowl to Poppy. "I had to go to the mall today, and the Santa Claus was wearing shorts."

Mr. Foreman nodded. He piled a heap of spaghetti onto his plate. "On the way home, I passed a yard where they put Christmas lights on their palm trees."

"I guess we won't have a white Christmas this year," Reggie said, wiping spaghetti sauce off his chin.

"Why did we have to leave Ohio?" Poppy grumbled. She passed the salad bowl to her dad without taking any.

Her dad frowned. "Do I really have to say it again? The office moved my job to Tampa, remember?"

"Wipe that look off your face, Poppy," Mom scolded. "You didn't love Cleveland that much, either. You complained that you had to wear three sweaters at a time. You were always so cold."

"I did it because layers are cool," Poppy muttered into her spaghetti. "Not because I was cold."

Reggie watched his sister across the table. Still angry. Jabbing her fork into her plate like a weapon. They didn't talk about the Holiday Talent Show yesterday. But he knew it was still on her mind and making her grumpy.

That morning, he had stopped at her bedroom door. "Hey, Poppy," he said. "I had an idea. Want me to give you a few pointers on the banjo?"

She said some very rude words and slammed the door in his face.

He stared at the door. "I guess that's a no?"

After breakfast, he had tried again to pull her out of her bad mood. "I'm going to the skate park with Diego. Want to come along?"

She growled at him. "Should I tell you what you can do with your skateboard?"

Poppy could have a mean mouth when she was angry.

Reggie and Diego had gone to the skate park that afternoon and had a great time. They met some guys and picked up a few new tricks and survived without a single scrape or scratch.

Reggie loved wearing shorts and a T-shirt in December. Who needed gloves and snow parkas and clunky boots?

How could Poppy be so down on Florida?

Now dinner was nearly over, and she was still grumpy.

"Is that all you're going to eat?" their mom asked, staring at the pile of spaghetti on Poppy's plate.

"Are you keeping track?" Poppy snapped. "Do you want to count the strands?"

"Can I remind you that it's almost Christmas?" their dad said, his eyes on Poppy. "That's probably the best time of year to be nice to your parents. Don't you think?"

Poppy didn't reply.

"I think I know what you should get Poppy for Christmas," Reggie said.

"A muzzle?" their mom suggested.

It wasn't a very nice joke, but they all laughed. Even Poppy.

"A new banjo," Reggie said. "My old banjo is garbage. And Poppy could be really awesome with a new one."

Poppy banged her fork on the table so hard the plate jumped. "I don't *want* a banjo!" she said through gritted teeth. "I don't want to talk about banjos. I hate the banjo. I'm never going to play it again. It's a stupid instrument."

"Just because a string broke—" Reggie started.

"Shut up about the banjo," Poppy growled. "I mean it." She scooted her chair back and started to stand up.

"Sit down." Mr. Foreman waved her down with both hands. "Let's talk about what you *do* want for Christmas."

"This should be a *fun* conversation," their mom said. "Not an argument."

"Who's arguing?" Poppy said, crossing her arms in front of her.

Reggie tossed a dinner roll across the table at his sister. It bounced off her forehead and onto her plate. Poppy didn't react at all. She just stared straight ahead.

His mom squinted at him. "Why did you do that?"

Reggie shrugged. "I don't know. I just felt like it."

Even though it was kind of mean, everyone thought it was funny. Poppy tried not to laugh, but a small smile crossed her face.

"I had this cool idea," Reggie told his parents. "Wouldn't it be funny if Junior had a dummy of his own? You could buy me a little tiny one to put on Junior's lap. I'd call him Junior Junior. It would be a riot!"

"Funny idea—" Mr. Foreman started.

But Poppy interrupted. "*I'm* the one who likes puppets and dolls. Not Reggie. I've always been the one. Look at all the old dolls in my closet. I used to make them talk and put on shows—remember?"

"True," their dad said. "But, so what does that mean?"

"So I want a ventriloquist dummy for Christmas!" Poppy shouted. "I want a dummy of my own."

And that's when all the scary stuff started.

"Poppy, you're copying me again," Reggie said.

"I am not!" she cried. "I really want a dummy I can perform with. Maybe I'll do kids' birthday parties with it, and parents will pay me to entertain." She scowled at him and narrowed her eyes to slits. "Why should *you* always get all the attention?"

"You shouldn't be jealous of Reggie," their mother said. "He found something he really enjoys, and he's good at it."

Poppy shook her head. "I'm not jealous. I just want a dummy. They sell them at Sackler's toy store. You know. That store we went to after the Buccaneers game? Across from the football stadium?" She crossed her arms again. "What's the big deal?"

"The big deal is," Reggie said, "that you're copying me again. Why can't you do your own thing?"

"Why don't you shut up?" Poppy snapped. "You're just afraid I'll be better at it than you!"

"Stop it, you two!" Mr. Foreman said. "I'll buy you a dummy, Poppy. But you two can't be fighting about it all the time."

"And you can't be competing over them," their mom added.

"We're not fighting," Reggie said. He turned to his sister. "Okay, if you get a dummy, I'll help you with it. I'll show you how to throw your voice and work his eyes and mouth. And I'll help you with your jokes and stuff."

"That's nice of you, Reggie," their dad said.

"Your brother always tries to help you," Mrs. Foreman said. "He helped you with the banjo, too. And with your skateboard, although you gave that up, too."

"But I don't *need* his help," Poppy insisted. She turned to her dad. "The dummy is called Mister Wood. I saw boxes and boxes of Mister Wood dummies at Sackler's. That's the one I want."

Mr. Foreman lifted the dinner napkin off his lap and dropped it onto the table. He smiled. "Well, Poppy. Maybe Santa will bring it to you."

And that was that.

It won't be long now, readers. Mister Wood will be appearing soon. And—trust me—the Foreman household will never be the same.

It was Christmas morning in Tampa. The sun was already high in the sky, and the air was summer warm. From his window Reggie saw a few seagulls soaring above the trees.

Poppy and his mom and dad were already downstairs. His parents were sitting in front of the unlit fireplace in their robes with large coffee mugs in their hands. Poppy was still in her *My Little Pony* pajamas, which Grandma Florence had bought her.

The family didn't have a Christmas tree this year. Instead, the brightly wrapped presents were scattered on the floor in front of the mantel.

"Hey, good morning," Reggie said, still wiping the sleep from his eyes. "I think I see my present."

It was easy to spot because it wasn't wrapped. Reggie hurried across the room and lifted it in both hands. "That's it!" he said. "The exact boogie board I had my eyes on!"

Reggie rubbed the slick, shiny surface. It was a forty-two-inch bodyboard, magenta with blue waves rolling across it. He had studied bodyboards online for weeks, and this was his first choice.

"I can't believe you found this one!" he said. He hugged his mom, then his dad, causing them to almost spill their coffee.

Poppy jumped up from the couch and took the board from Reggie's hands. The board was nearly as tall as she was. "I could ride this," she told Reggie. "Can I go with you when you go to the beach?"

"I just got it, and you already want it," Reggie grumbled.

"No. I just want to try it," Poppy replied. "I'm a better swimmer than you. I'll be awesome with this."

"Who taught you how to swim?" Reggie demanded.

"I did! Remember? You were afraid to let go of the side of the pool. And I showed you—"

"Stop, you two," their dad said, rubbing his forehead. "It's too early in the morning for this."

"Poppy, don't you want to open your big present?" Mrs. Foreman asked.

Poppy stepped over to the large box leaning against the wall. It was wrapped in sparkly, silver-and-red paper, with a silvery bow tied to the front. "This is it, right?" she said.

She didn't wait for an answer. She pulled off the

bow and tossed it on the floor. Then she began ripping the paper off. When the wrapping was half off, she could see the big yellow words on the box: MEET MISTER WOOD.

"You got it! You got it for me!" Poppy cried, jumping up and down. She frantically clawed the rest of the wrapping paper away and held the large box in both hands.

She tried to pry open the top, but it was taped shut.

"Read the box first," her dad said. "What does it say?"

Poppy raised the front of the box and read out loud: *"MEET MISTER WOOD. He's your funny friend. Learn to throw your voice and become a ventriloquist. Amaze your audience! Mister Wood makes it EASY and FUN!"*

"Remember, I can help you with him, if you want," Reggie said. "I'll show you some tricks for working the eyes and the mouth."

"No, I want to do it myself," Poppy said. She held the box up to her dad. "Can you help me get the lid open? It's taped."

Mr. Foreman strode to the kitchen and returned a few seconds later with a pair of scissors. He cut the tape, and Poppy pulled the dummy from the box.

Reggie laughed. "He's ugly! He's not cute like Junior."

"*I* think he's cute," Poppy insisted.

The dummy had black hair painted on its wooden head. Large dark eyes. A wide grin with red lips. Poppy straightened its red bow tie. "Hi, Mister Wood," she said. "I think you're *very* cute!"

She held him up for her parents. "Isn't he awesome?"

"We're glad you like him," her mom said.

Reggie laughed again. "He's weird-looking. And everyone will have that same dummy. The toy stores sell boxes and boxes of Mister Woods. At least Junior is one of a kind."

Poppy stuck her tongue out at him. "Who cares?" she snapped. "Mister Wood and I are going to be best friends. I'm going to think up some awesome jokes for him. And I'm going to be a great ventriloquist."

Reggie raised both hands in surrender. "Okay, okay. I just wanted to help." He was starting to get fed up with his sister. Time after time, he tried to be nice to her. But . . . why bother? She was only mean back.

Poppy turned and walked up the stairs to her room. She sat Mister Wood down in the chair beside her bed. Then she crossed the room to her closet to change out of her pajamas.

She didn't see the dummy blink his eyes and turn his head from side to side.

If she had, she might have been scared.

Reggie and his family had Christmas dinner at their Aunt Halley's house. Poppy insisted on bringing Mister Wood.

Reggie didn't know exactly how old Aunt Halley was. But he knew she was pretty old. She dyed her hair bright red, and she wore red dresses and always had a red scarf around her neck, which she tied and untied while she talked.

She was always chattering away, pinching the kids' cheeks, teasing them, asking a dozen questions and not even waiting for the answers. She never sat still for more than two minutes.

Aunt Halley greeted them at her front door and shoved cups of hot cider into their hands before they even had their coats off. "This is my favorite holiday," she said, "because it matches my house."

Just about everything in Aunt Halley's house was red and green. The walls were red with green trim.

The living room couches were green, and the coffee table was red.

"It's like you live in a Christmas ornament!" Reggie declared.

Everyone laughed. Halley pinched Reggie's cheek, leaving a red mark.

She turned to Poppy, who was clutching Mister Wood. "Did you get that doll for Christmas? Aren't you getting a little old for dolls?"

"It's not a doll," Poppy told her. "It's a ventriloquist dummy. His name is Mister Wood, and I'm going to do an act with him and make money at birthday parties."

Aunt Halley shook the dummy's wooden hand up and down. "Nice to meet you, Mister Wood."

"Touch me again and I'll spit!" Mister Wood cried.

Aunt Halley gasped. "Poppy, why do you have to make Mister Wood so rude? Is that your idea of comedy?"

Poppy's mouth dropped open. "I—I didn't say that, Aunt Halley. The dummy said it. I swear. It wasn't me!"

"Poppy—say you're sorry," her mom said.

"But . . ." Poppy stared at the dummy. "I'm telling the truth. I didn't say it." She turned to Reggie. Her expression changed. She pointed a finger at him. "Oh. I get it. *You* made him say that. You threw your voice to trick us."

Reggie raised both hands and backed away. "Don't

look at me. It wasn't me. We all know it had to be you, Poppy."

"That dummy has an odd grin," Aunt Halley said. "Very disturbing."

"*Your face is disturbing ME!*" Mister Wood said in a high, shrill voice.

"Stop it, Poppy!" Mr. Foreman snapped. "I'm serious. Just because you have a dummy doesn't give you an excuse to insult your aunt."

"But—but—" Poppy sputtered. "I—I didn't! I—"

Reggie laughed. "I saw you move your lips. You're not a very good ventriloquist yet."

"Listen to me. I didn't say those things," Poppy cried.

Aunt Halley studied the dummy. "He's kind of ugly," she said.

"*You should know!*" Mister Wood snickered.

"Enough!" Poppy's dad said.

"I . . . I have to put him down," Poppy said. Her voice trembled. "There's something weird going on here."

Mrs. Foreman put her hands on Reggie's shoulders and turned him around to face her. "Tell me the truth. Are you the one saying those awful things?"

"No way," Reggie said. "Really, Mom." He made a zipping motion over his mouth with one hand. "My lips have been sealed."

Poppy crossed the room and sat the dummy on a low

stool against the wall. "Weird," she muttered. "This is so totally weird."

Aunt Halley passed around a large tray of cheese and crackers. "Where did you get that dummy?" she asked.

"At Sackler's," Mr. Foreman replied. "They had a big stack of Mister Wood dolls. The guy told me they sold twenty of them this Christmas."

Aunt Halley laughed. "I hope they're not all as rude as this one." She disappeared into the kitchen to check on dinner.

Poppy sat on the edge of the couch, staring at the dummy.

Reggie felt confused. *Why did Poppy make the dummy say those things to Aunt Halley?* he wondered. *Was she trying to get me in trouble? Everyone knows I'm good at throwing my voice. Did Poppy think I'd get blamed?*

Reggie wanted to talk to his sister. But Aunt Halley had returned from the kitchen and was asking them questions about what they were doing in school, and what they got for Christmas, and what their New Year's resolutions were.

When they sat down at the dining room table, Poppy was way at the far end, so Reggie couldn't talk to her then, either. But his mind spun with questions.

Why did Poppy insist the dummy was talking on

his own? No one would ever believe that. What was she trying to do?

"Mmmmmm. The food smells so good!" Mr. Foreman exclaimed.

From the living room came a raspy voice. *"Smells like something I stepped in!"*

"It's late," Mr. Foreman said as the family walked into their house through the kitchen. "I think it's after eleven."

"It's hard to leave Halley's," Mrs. Foreman said. "We spent half an hour just saying good-bye."

"My ribs are sore from all her hugs," Reggie murmured.

Poppy yawned. She carried Mister Wood over her shoulder.

"Great dinner," their dad said. "Halley is a great cook." He turned to Poppy. "So what's up with this dummy? Why did you make him say those insulting things? That's not like you, Poppy."

"I don't want to talk about it," she replied. She yawned again. "I'm going to bed."

Mr. Foreman stopped her with a hand on her shoulder. "You have no explanation?"

"No. I don't," Poppy muttered. "Ask Mister Wood."

She sighed. "I told you I didn't say those things. But you don't want to believe me."

"Of course we don't believe you. I don't like this attitude," he said. "What you did wasn't funny, and you know it."

Poppy sighed again. "It had to be Reggie throwing his voice. You know he's been practicing that for months."

"No way!" Reggie shouted. "No *way* I would do that. Take that back, Poppy. You're wrong. You're totally wrong!"

She rolled her eyes. "Okay. I hear you. Can I go to bed now?"

She stomped into the living room. The dummy bounced on her shoulder as she started up the stairs.

"Goodnight, everyone," a shrill voice called.

"I didn't say that!" Poppy cried. "This is too weird." She returned to the living room and tossed the dummy onto the couch. "He can stay here tonight. He's creeping me out."

"No. No way. Take him upstairs and put him in your closet," Mr. Foreman insisted. "Your joking isn't funny."

"I'm not joking," she replied. But she grabbed Mister Wood and carried him upstairs.

Mr. Foreman turned to Reggie. "What's up with your sister?"

Reggie shrugged. "Beats me. She's really getting on my nerves."

"Why don't you talk to her tomorrow?" Mrs. Foreman said. "Find out why she keeps saying rude things and blaming it on you and that dummy. It's just so strange."

Reggie snickered. "Yeah. Poppy is strange."

"Well, this was still a great Christmas," Reggie's mom said to him. "Come here. Let me give you a Christmas hug."

"Oh no!" Reggie backed away. "No more hugs, Mom. Aunt Halley squeezed me like an accordion all day! I think I have at least two broken bones!"

His parents laughed. Mrs. Foreman gave him a push toward the stairs. "Okay, fine. No hug. Go to bed."

Reggie made his way up to his room. He changed into his pajamas and sat down on the edge of his bed. He thought about Poppy and her dummy.

Why is she trying to convince us the dummy is alive? She can't really believe it. Is it just a joke she's playing on us? Poppy is acting really strange—even for Poppy.

He didn't feel sleepy. He pulled out his phone and called Diego. Diego answered on the third ring. "Did I wake you up?" Reggie asked.

"No," Diego replied in a whisper. "I'm supposed to be asleep, but I'm playing *Minecraft.*"

Diego was obsessed with *Minecraft.* He constructed entire towns. Last week, he showed Reggie an amazing rollercoaster he had built.

"What did you get for Christmas?" Reggie asked.

"A bunch of clothes," Diego said. "My parents couldn't get the new PlayStation, so they got me clothes instead."

Reggie told him about his new boogie board and some other gifts he got. Then he said, "And guess what my parents gave Poppy? A Mister Wood dummy."

"Whaaaat?" Diego replied in surprise. "I didn't know she liked dummies."

"Tell me about it," Reggie said. "You know Poppy. She's a total copycat. So she had to have a dummy of her own because I have one. And, believe it or not, she's trying to tell us that her dummy is alive!"

"Excuse me?"

"Yeah," Reggie said. "She keeps saying the dummy is talking on his own."

Diego snorted. "Your sister is weird. Know what would be a riot, though?" he asked. "Why don't you make her believe her dummy is alive? For real."

Reggie moved the phone to his other ear. "I don't get it."

"Freak her out. Move the dummy to a different room. Make her think he can walk around. Pretend you actually believe that he talks on his own. Pretend you're scared of him, too."

Reggie laughed. "Diego, that's so mean! I would never think of anything like that."

Diego laughed, too. "Poppy deserves it—right?"

"I guess," Reggie replied. "I don't know. I don't like to scare my little sister. But . . . maybe it would teach her a lesson."

He said good-bye to Diego and shut off his phone.

Reggie thought about his friend's idea.

Maybe it isn't too mean. Maybe it'll be funny.

I think I'll try Diego's little joke right now, he decided.

Reggie walked to his bedroom door. He glanced at Junior, his dummy, grinning at him from his perch on a bookshelf. The dummy had tilted to one side. Reggie straightened him up.

Then Reggie made his way quietly down the hall to his sister's room. He peered in through the open door. The lights were off. Pale yellow light washed in from a streetlight at the bottom of the front yard.

He waited in the doorway for his eyes to adjust to the dimness. Poppy was asleep in her bed with the covers pulled up to her chin. The Mister Wood dummy lay facedown at the foot of the bed.

Reggie held his breath. Walking on tiptoes, he crept over the carpet and carefully, silently, lifted Mister Wood off the bed. Carrying the dummy in front of him, he tiptoed back out into the hall.

He glanced back into the room. Poppy hadn't moved. *Where should I hide him?* Reggie asked himself. He stopped in front of the linen closet. Should he stuff the dummy in with the sheets and blankets?

No. Poppy would know right away that Reggie had done it.

Reggie moved on to the guest room. *Perfect,* he thought. He turned on the light and carried the dummy to the bed. He sat Mister Wood on the quilt and leaned him against the pillows. He crossed the dummy's arms in front of him.

Awesome. He looks totally comfortable.

Reggie closed the guest room door. He pictured the puzzled look on Poppy's face when she woke up the next morning and saw that Mister Wood wasn't there.

It took Reggie a long time to fall asleep. He kept chuckling over his little joke.

The next morning, he was awakened by the sweet aroma of pancakes floating up to his room. Reggie ran downstairs in his pajamas and into the kitchen.

Mr. Foreman and Poppy were already at the kitchen table. Reggie's mom stood at the stove, flipping the pancakes in a big skillet.

"You're not funny!" Poppy shouted as soon as Reggie stepped into the room. "Where did you put Mister Wood?"

"Huh?" Reggie blinked his eyes several times and rubbed them, pretending to be still half asleep. "What are you talking about?"

"You know!" Poppy said. "Just tell me where you put him."

"Reggie." His mom turned from the stove. "Did you take Poppy's dummy from her room last night?"

Reggie blinked some more. "Who? Me? Of course not."

"Not a funny joke," his dad said, half hidden behind his coffee mug. "It's kind of a dumb prank, Reggie."

"Tell the truth," Poppy said, scowling at him. "You sneaked into my room and stole Mister Wood."

Reggie slid into his chair. He took a long sip of orange juice. "Why would I do that?"

"Because you're a jerk?" Poppy snapped.

Mrs. Foreman carried a platter of pancakes to the table. "Come on. Can we just have a nice breakfast?"

"Are we going to have dummy trouble the whole Christmas break?" their dad demanded. "I warned you two—"

His mom slid two pancakes onto Reggie's plate. Reggie inhaled their sweet smell, then reached for the syrup bottle. He grinned at Poppy. "You said your dummy was alive. Maybe he got up and walked away."

"I didn't say he was alive," Poppy shot back. "I just said—"

Mr. Foreman cleared his throat loudly to stop the argument. "Reggie, after breakfast you will go upstairs with your sister and help her find her dummy, okay?

53

And I don't want any more arguing about this for the rest of the vacation."

Reggie shrugged. "Sure. No problem," he said, chewing loudly. Syrup dripped down his chin, but he didn't wipe it away.

Poppy stared hard at him all through breakfast. When they were finished, they walked upstairs together. "How could you do that?" Poppy demanded.

Reggie kept a straight face. "Do what?"

"You must think I'm totally stupid. Did you really think I'd believe Mister Wood walked away on his own?"

Reggie shrugged. "How do I know what you think?"

"Just get him," Poppy said.

"He has to be up here somewhere," Reggie said, pretending to search. He opened the linen closet. They both gazed up and down the shelves. "No. Not in here."

"Did you hide him somewhere in *your* room?" Poppy asked.

Reggie shook his head. "No way."

They stopped at the guest room door. Poppy pushed it open. They both stepped inside. Poppy stared at the figure on the bed.

"Hey, wait—!" Reggie cried. His breath caught in his throat. "What's up with this?"

Junior sat against the pillows, his arms crossed, his eyes wide.

"What's Junior doing in here?" Poppy asked him.

"I . . . I don't know," Reggie stammered. He pushed Poppy out of the way and hurtled down the hall to his bedroom. As he burst into the room, his eyes stopped on the bookshelf.

"Huh?" Reggie uttered a startled gasp. Mister Wood, a wide grin on his red wooden lips, sat on the shelf in the exact place where he always kept Junior.

Poppy rushed forward and pulled Mister Wood off the shelf. "Why did you do that, Reggie?" she demanded. "Why did you put my dummy up there?"

"I . . . I didn't," Reggie stammered. "I swear."

"I don't get it," Poppy said, shaking her head. "Did you think I wouldn't find him?"

"I'm telling you, I didn't put him there!" Reggie shouted.

He had a sudden thought. "It was you—wasn't it? You put Junior in the guest room and moved your dummy to my bookshelf."

He was certain that Poppy had sneaked into his room while he was still asleep this morning and made the switch. If he had looked at his bookshelf before he went down for breakfast, he was sure he would have seen it.

"Don't be stupid," Poppy shot back. "Why would I do that?"

Mr. Foreman appeared behind them. "Is there a problem here?"

"No," they both replied at once. "But Reggie moved my dummy," Poppy said.

"Poppy moved the dummies," Reggie said.

Their dad held his hands against his ears. "I don't want to hear about it. No dummy trouble. Do you understand?"

They both nodded. Poppy carried Mister Wood to her room. She planned to practice new jokes with him.

"What are you doing this morning?" Reggie's dad asked him.

"Going over to Diego's to check out his presents."

"Well, don't forget your cousin Jake's party this afternoon, Reggie. Tell you what—why don't you meet us there?"

"No problem," Reggie said. In his room, he tucked Junior back on the bookshelf. He crossed to the bathroom and brushed his teeth.

Poppy got me this time, he thought, shaking his head. *I tried to trick her. But the joke was on me.*

He changed into shorts and a T-shirt, and headed to Diego's house down the block.

The day after Christmas, it was seventy-five degrees and not a cloud in the clear blue sky. Reggie wondered if he'd ever get used to Christmastime in Florida.

At Diego's house, he found his friend in his room. Diego wore a new *Minecraft* T-shirt his parents had given him for Christmas. He was on the floor with his laptop, watching puppy-training videos on YouTube.

"Check this one out," he said as Reggie stepped into the room. "'How to Get Your Dog to Stop Chewing Things.'"

Reggie laughed. "I don't get it. Did you get a dog for Christmas?"

Diego shook his head. "Nope. My parents are allergic to dogs."

Reggie sat down beside him on the floor. "Then why are you watching training videos?"

"I don't know," Diego said. "I just like them. They're kind of cool."

That was one of the things Reggie liked about Diego. He was into a lot of things, and he couldn't really explain why.

The little dog on Diego's laptop monitor was chewing on a leg of a coffee table. "Think you might want to be a dog trainer someday?" Reggie asked.

"No. I want to be a video game tester," Diego replied. "You know, they pay people a lot of money for that."

"Awesome," Reggie said.

Diego paused the video. "Hey, how'd it go last night with your sister's Mister Wood dummy? Did you move it? Did she freak out when she saw it was missing?"

Reggie sighed. "It didn't go well. It didn't go well at all."

"Did you move her dummy?"

Reggie nodded. "Yeah. But Poppy pulled a double twist on me. I'm not sure when she did it . . . Maybe when I was asleep. But she switched the two dummies. She put them in different rooms. Then she blamed *me* for moving them."

Diego laughed. "Your sister is pretty awesome."

"No, she isn't," Reggie said. "She's annoying."

"I think you should keep trying," Diego said.

"Keep trying what?"

"To make Poppy think the dummy is alive," Diego replied. He reached for a bag of potato chips beside him on the floor and offered some to Reggie.

"You mean move him again?"

Diego nodded. "Yeah. Move him every night. And swear that you didn't do it."

"That's boring," Reggie said. He reached for another handful of chips. "And she'll never believe it wasn't me."

Diego thought for a long moment. "I've got it. When she goes out, mess up her room. Take all her clothes out of the dresser drawers and throw them on the floor. Then sit the Mister Wood dummy down on top of the pile."

Reggie rolled his eyes. "How will *that* work? She'll just say that I did it, and I'll get in major trouble."

"No. It could work," Diego said. Reggie could see that his friend was thinking hard, excited about the plan.

Diego grabbed his shoulder. "Listen to me. You sneak home. Don't let anyone see you. Mess up Poppy's room and then hurry back here. Then you can say you were here at my house the whole time. And you couldn't have made the mess."

"I won't have to sneak," Reggie said. "They won't be home. I'm meeting them at my cousin Jake's house."

"Perfect," Diego said. "You'll see. You'll get Poppy this time."

Reggie bumped fists with Diego. "You really are some kind of evil genius."

Diego chuckled. "For sure."

Reggie hurried home a little after two. He knew that his mom and dad and Poppy were already at Jake's house. The coast would be clear. Time for a little dummy mischief.

He stepped into the house through the back door and hurried to the stairs.

"Hey—you're home!" a voice called.

Reggie practically jumped out of his skin.

Mrs. Foreman stepped into the hallway. "I was just about to call you," she said.

"Oh. Uh. Really?" Reggie stammered. "I thought I was going to meet you—"

His mom strode across the front entryway to him. "We're running late. Now we can all go together." She shook her head. "Can you believe it's Jake's fourteenth birthday?"

Jake's birthday was the day after Christmas. Could there be a worse time to have a birthday? Jake always got combination birthday-Christmas presents, half the presents a kid should get!

"As long as you're here, go upstairs and change your shirt," she told him. "We have to dress up for Jake's party. Why don't you wear that nice button-down shirt I bought you for Christmas? You know. The blue one."

"Oh. Okay," Reggie replied. His heart was still pounding from the surprise of finding his family at home. He stopped halfway up the stairs. "I don't know where it is."

"I'll come up and show you and help you take the pins out," Mrs. Foreman said. She followed him up the stairs.

They made their way to Reggie's room and pushed open the door. Reggie clicked on the ceiling light.

"Oh no!" his mother cried. "What happened in here?"

Reggie pushed past her and stumbled over to his bed. It took him a while to believe what he was seeing.

Poppy's Mister Wood dummy sat up straight in the middle of Reggie's bed. The dummy held a pair of scissors in front of him in one wooden hand. And draped over the dummy's lap was Reggie's new blue shirt.

Cut into ribbons.

Reggie froze at the side of the bed and stared. *Am I dreaming this?* he wondered.

The shirt had been snipped into long strips. One blue strip was caught in the scissors. The dummy grinned at Reggie, his eyes wide, as if he was proud of what he had done.

Reggie's mom stepped up behind him. She grabbed the ruined shirt off the bed and shook it in the air. "No . . . no . . . no . . ." she repeated. "This isn't right. How *could* she?"

Holding the shirt in front of her, she turned back to

the door and shouted: "Poppy! Are you in your room? Poppy? Get in here! This minute!"

Reggie heard footsteps in the hall. A few seconds later, his sister appeared in the bedroom doorway. "Hey—what's up?" Poppy said.

Then she saw the cut-up strips in her mother's hands.

Poppy's eyes went wide, and her mouth dropped open. "Oh no," she murmured. "What's *that*?"

Mrs. Foreman shook the shirt. "It's your brother's Christmas shirt," she said through gritted teeth. "How could you do this, Poppy? How *could* you?"

Poppy took a step back into the hall. "Huh? Me?" she cried.

"Why?" her mother demanded angrily. "Tell me. Why? What on earth possessed you to destroy a brand-new shirt?"

"I . . . I didn't!" Poppy cried. "You don't really think I did that—do you?"

"I sure don't think the *dummy* did it!" Mrs. Foreman cried.

"But I never—" Poppy started.

Reggie took the shirt from his mother and held it up. "I don't get it, Poppy," he said. "Why are you trying to make us believe your dummy is alive? I don't get the joke. Why are you doing this?"

"I . . . I didn't do it!" Poppy stammered. "I would never do something like that." She stared at the ripped-up shirt. Her expression changed. "Oh, I get it," she said, narrowing her eyes at her brother. "*You* did it—didn't you, Reggie? You cut up your own shirt to get me in trouble!"

"That's not true!" Reggie screamed. "I was at Diego's house. I wasn't even here. How can you think—"

"You didn't want me to have a dummy of my own," Poppy cried. "You always have to be the star—don't you? So you did this to your shirt to get me in trouble so Mom and Dad would take Mister Wood away from me!"

"No way!" Reggie shouted. "No way! No way!"

Mrs. Foreman stepped between them. "Enough!" she said. "I mean it, you two. That's enough."

"You can't blame me—" Poppy started.

Her mother raised a finger to her lips. "Silence. Poppy, your brother was at Diego's house all morning. You were the only one home. So I have no choice but to think you were the one who destroyed his shirt."

"But—but—but—" Poppy sputtered.

"You will have to pay for it from your allowance," Mrs. Foreman said. "Cutting up a shirt is *twisted*. This dummy war has to stop right now. Do you understand?"

Poppy lowered her eyes but didn't reply.

"Now, get changed. Both of you," their mother said. "Hurry. We're going to be late to your cousin Jake's party."

Poppy muttered something under her breath. She

slumped out the door. Her mother followed, shaking her head. Reggie went to his closet to find a clean shirt.

None of them saw the Mister Wood dummy sit up in the bed and wink.

Well, readers, how long will it take Reggie and Poppy to figure out what is really going on here?

I don't want to give it away.

But let me just tell you—things are going to get a *lot* worse before they get better.

17

Reggie liked his cousin Jake. But his birthday party wasn't much fun. For one thing, there weren't any other kids there. Just some aunts and uncles and their friends. And since it was the day after Christmas, they all seemed pretty tired and not in a partying mood.

Reggie was happy to get home, head to his room to change into his pajamas, and go to bed. He found the cut-up blue shirt on his bed, a reminder of the unpleasant afternoon. How could Poppy go so far overboard?

He balled it up and stuffed it into the wastebasket beside his desk. Junior, his dummy, grinned at him from his place on the bookshelf against the wall.

Reggie yawned. He thought about texting Diego and telling him about Mister Wood with the scissors in his hand, the new Christmas shirt cut into pieces, and Poppy pretending she didn't cut it.

But it was late, and he felt sleepy. The story could wait until tomorrow.

The bedroom window was open. A warm breeze made the curtains rustle. Reggie settled into the darkness and was just drifting off to sleep when he felt a hand on his shoulder.

"Huh?" He blinked himself alert and sat up with a startled cry. He squinted up at Poppy, who leaned over him.

"Reggie, are you asleep?" she whispered.

"Not anymore," he murmured. He turned and lowered his feet to the floor. "What do you want, Poppy? What are you doing in here?"

"I . . . I'm scared," she stammered.

He frowned at her. "Scared? Scared of *what*?"

"Listen to me." She grabbed his shoulder again. "Stop being angry and listen, okay?"

He nodded. Even in the dim light, he could see the fear on her face.

She dropped beside him on the edge of the bed. The curtains blew into the room, and the warm, damp breeze washed over them.

"Can we talk for real?" she asked, her voice just above a whisper. "I mean, can we be honest with each other?"

"Sure," Reggie said. His eyes locked on hers. What was troubling her?

"You know I didn't cut up your shirt," she said. "You know I would never do anything like that. Right?"

He didn't reply.

"Well, I didn't do it," Poppy continued. "And I know you didn't do it, either. I just said that to Mom before because . . . because I didn't know what to say."

Reggie groaned. "So you're going to tell me that Mister Wood did it? You woke me up with that same story?"

"Just listen to me," Poppy insisted. "I know you think I'm making it up. But I'm scared, Reggie. If you and I didn't cut up that shirt . . . who did?"

"Poppy, give me a break."

"And on Christmas at Aunt Halley's? I really didn't say those horrible things," Poppy whispered. "I really thought you did it. That's not even my sense of humor."

She tugged on his pajama sleeve. "Come on. Try to believe me. I really am scared. I don't know if he's alive or not, but—"

"That only happens in movies," Reggie said, pushing her hand away. "Let's get real here."

"I . . . I closed Mister Wood up in my closet," Poppy stammered.

Reggie squinted at her. "You *what*?"

"I stuffed him in there and shut the door. I didn't know what else to do. I really am frightened of him. I think he's watching me. And that sick grin on his face . . ."

"Is this another trick you're playing?" Reggie demanded.

Poppy raised her right hand. "I swear."

Poppy really does look upset, Reggie thought.

"Okay. Don't be scared. Let me come and take a good look at him," Reggie said. "I'm sure you've just worked yourself up for no reason."

"I know I'm being weird. But—"

Poppy tugged Reggie to his feet. "Okay, okay. Don't pull me. I'm coming."

He straightened his pajama bottoms and followed her out into the hall. A night-light near the floor cast a pale glow over the dark rug. The floorboards creaked beneath their feet. Their dad always talked about replacing them. But he hadn't gotten around to it.

Poppy stopped at the doorway to her bedroom and clicked on the ceiling light. Blinking in the sudden brightness, Reggie followed her into the room.

They both stopped and stared at the same time.

The closet door stood wide open.

"No! It can't be!" Poppy pressed her hands to her cheeks and stared wide eyed at the open closet door.

Reggie hesitated for a moment. Then he darted across the room and peered into the closet. "Not here," he said. "No dummy in here."

"I . . . I put him on the floor . . . against the back wall," Poppy stammered. She stood back, watching her brother, afraid to approach the closet.

Reggie turned and studied her. He could see that she wasn't pulling a prank. She was trembling and pale, genuinely frightened.

"He . . . got out," Poppy said. "He's somewhere in the house."

She finally worked up the courage to step over to the closet. Reggie backed away, and Poppy peered in. She turned on the closet light. Her shirts and jeans and dresses hadn't been touched. A pile of dirty clothes was heaped on the floor behind her sneakers.

No sign of Mister Wood.

Poppy backed out of the closet and dropped onto the edge of her bed. Reggie shivered despite the warmth of the night. Hugging himself, he moved beside Poppy.

"We'd better wake up Mom and Dad and tell them," he said.

Poppy shrugged. "What good would that do? No way they'd ever believe us."

"This can't be happening," Reggie said. "They sell *hundreds* of Mister Wood dummies. Dad said they had a big stack of them at Sackler's. Someone would have told Sackler if they were alive. It's impossible!"

Poppy jumped to her feet. "We've got to find him. He has to be around here somewhere."

They both started for the door—then stopped.

A floorboard creaked.

A soft footstep thumped in the hall. A scrape. A quiet *thud*. Another squeak of a floorboard.

"He . . . he's out there," Poppy whispered. "He's coming . . ."

They both stared at the doorway.

Another creak. Closer. Another soft *thud* of a footstep.

Why is he trying to sneak up on us? Reggie wondered. *What is he going to do?*

The light in the hall turned to shadow. The figure stepped into the doorway.

And both kids screamed.

"Dad!" Poppy cried. She jumped to her feet. "We thought—"

"Dad—it's you!" Reggie said.

"Who were you expecting?" Mr. Foreman demanded. "Frosty the Snowman?" He tied his bathrobe tighter around himself and stepped into the room. "What's going on up here? Your mom and I could hear you from downstairs."

"It . . . it's the dummy!" Poppy cried.

Her father raised a hand. "No. Don't start! I'm serious. I don't want to hear anything about either of your dummies." He peered around Poppy's room. "Where *is* your dummy? I hope you put him away somewhere."

"That's just it, Dad," Poppy replied. "I did put him away. In the closet. And—"

"It's late and we're all tired from Christmas and all the parties," he said. "So why are you two still up? And why are you talking about those dummies?"

Poppy balled her hands into fists at her sides. "If you'll just let me explain—"

"You've got to listen to her, Dad," Reggie spoke up. "Something weird is going on."

"The only weird things around here are you two," Mr. Foreman grumbled. He pressed his hands against his waist. "Go ahead. Tell me what you want to tell me." He yawned. "This better be good."

"It . . . it isn't good," Poppy stammered. "I put Mister Wood away in my closet. I was kind of freaked out. So I closed him up in there. And look." She pointed to the open closet door. "He got out."

Mr. Foreman rubbed his forehead. "He got *out*? A wooden dummy escaped from your closet? Am I really hearing this? Am I having a nightmare? Or is this some kind of joke the two of you dreamed up?"

"No, Dad. Please—" Poppy pleaded. "Please believe me. Look in the closet. Go ahead. Look."

Mr. Foreman crossed to the closet and poked his head in. "Okay. No dummy in there. So what?"

"He's walking around somewhere in the house, Dad," Poppy said. "I don't know where. It . . . it's not a joke. I'm really scared."

Their dad studied them both for a long moment. Then he chuckled.

"Maybe the dummy is downstairs in the kitchen help-ing himself to leftover turkey. I hope so. I *hate* leftover turkey!"

"But—Dad—"

Reggie grabbed her arm. "Poppy, he's not going to believe you," he told his sister. "Better give it up."

"Good thinking," Mr. Foreman said. "Here's what I *do* believe. Any more dummy trouble of any kind, and Mister Wood goes back to the store."

He shook his head. "I thought it was a great gift, Poppy. You really wanted it, and I thought you could have a lot of fun with it. But that dummy has brought nothing but trouble to this family."

"But, Dad—"

He turned and started to the door. "Good night, you two," he said. "And if you happen to see Mister Wood walking by, tell him I said good night to him, too."

They listened to their dad thumping down the stairs. Poppy hugged herself and stared at the open closet door.

"Told you so," Reggie said. He yawned. "Why don't parents ever believe their kids?"

"I'm going to lock my door," Poppy said. "But I'll be up all night. I know I will."

"I'll leave my door open," he told her. "If you hear something weird, just shout and I'll come running."

She shivered. "Thanks, Reggie." *She really is*

scared, Reggie thought as she followed him to the door. He knew she was watching him walk down the hall to his room. He turned and saw her standing there for a moment, listening.

Silence.

Then she closed the bedroom door and locked it with a sharp *click*.

Reggie's head was spinning as he made his way back to his room. He felt tired and confused. He wanted to believe Poppy's story about the dummy escaping from the closet.

But how was it possible? Could Poppy be making the whole thing up after all?

But it definitely didn't seem like an act.

Reggie didn't know *what* to think. Right now, he wanted to go to sleep and not worry about anything till tomorrow.

He stepped into his room and saw at once that something was wrong.

What was that round object on the floor in front of the bed? He blinked, waiting for it to come into focus. And then he let out a sharp cry.

Junior's head?

He dropped to the rug and picked it up. Junior's wooden head. And beside the bed? An arm. A torn shirt sleeve with a dummy arm in it.

"Noooo!" Another cry escaped Reggie's throat.

The dummy's shoes lay under Reggie's desk chair. Next to them, a wooden hand.

His heart pounding, Reggie held Junior's head in his hands. He raised his gaze to the bed—and gasped. There was Mister Wood, sitting up straight, cross-legged, in the middle of Reggie's bed, grinning . . . grinning at Reggie.

And what was cupped in Mister Wood's hand? Reggie stood up and squinted to see better.

In Mister Wood's hand . . . Junior's eyeballs!

20

"It's lucky I saved the box," Mr. Foreman said. He lifted the Mister Wood dummy by the head and lowered him into the box. Then he carefully shut the lid.

Reggie, Poppy, and their mother looked on. Mrs. Foreman frowned at Poppy. "Do you have any explanation before your father returns the dummy to the toy store? Anything you'd like to say?"

Poppy shook her head. She kept her eyes down and muttered, "No. Not really."

"Do you want to apologize to your brother?" Mrs. Foreman demanded.

Poppy shrugged. "For what? I didn't do anything."

"You're still insisting you didn't wreck Reggie's dummy?" her mom asked.

Poppy kept her eyes down and didn't answer.

"Well, say good-bye to Mister Wood," their dad said. He finished packing up the dummy. "It certainly has been an unhappy Christmastime around here."

"Good riddance," Poppy muttered. "I never really wanted a dummy anyway." She turned and hurried up to her room.

"That dummy was bad news," Reggie said.

"Well, there will be a lot *less* bad news around here with that dummy out of the house," his mother said.

Mr. Foreman drove across town to Sackler's toy store. The store had just opened for the day, and a clerk was stacking video game boxes on a shelf behind the front counter.

He set the box down on the counter and waited for the clerk to turn around. The clerk was a young man with short copper-colored hair and bright blue eyes. He had a silver hoop in one ear. And he wore a black-and-red T-shirt with the name *Sackler's House of Toys* across the front.

"This is a return," Mr. Foreman said, patting the top of the box.

"Seriously?" the clerk said. "These are usually a big hit. Mister Wood was one of our bestsellers this holiday. After all the games and tech stuff, of course."

"Well, I need to return it," Mr. Foreman insisted. "Can I get a refund?"

"Let me see," the young man replied. He pried up the lid and pulled the dummy from the box. "Whoa."

He blinked a few times and studied the dummy up

and down. Then he turned to Mr. Foreman. "Sir, where is the dummy that came in this box?" he asked.

"Excuse me?" Mr. Foreman couldn't hide his confusion.

"This dummy didn't come in this box," the clerk explained. "This isn't a Mister Wood."

"Of course it is," Mr. Foreman replied. "I bought this here. This is the box. And this is the dummy that was in the box."

The clerk shook his head. "No way," he said. "I'll show you."

He set the dummy down on the counter and disappeared into a back room. Mr. Foreman stared at the dummy, sprawled on its back on the glass counter.

"You've *got* to be Mister Wood," he said to it. "That guy doesn't know what he's talking about."

The dummy stared back at him with his red-lipped grin.

The clerk returned a minute later carrying another Mister Wood box. "Look," he said. He set the box down and pulled open the lid. Then he lifted the dummy from the box.

"Weird," Mr. Foreman said, scratching his head. The Mister Wood from the box had red hair and freckles and wore black-framed eyeglasses. He was dressed in a checkered lumberjack shirt and bright red pants.

"They don't look anything alike!" Mr. Foreman exclaimed.

"I told you so," the clerk said. "Your dummy isn't Mister Wood. Someone must have switched dummies. They put this one in the Mister Wood box."

"But . . . why would anyone do that?" Mr. Foreman asked.

Both men uttered startled cries as the dummy on the counter suddenly sat up on his own. He tossed back his head, opened his mouth wide, and laughed.

"Say hi to Slappy!" the dummy cried in a shrill voice. "I'm a *baaaaad* boy!"

"N-no! No way!" the clerk stammered. "That didn't just happen." Eyes wide with fear, he raised both hands and backed away from the counter.

"This is impossible!" Mr. Foreman cried. He gaped at the dummy. "You can't talk!"

"Neither can *you*!" Slappy shrieked. He waved his hands in the air and shouted out a string of strange words.

Mr. Foreman's mouth locked open. His eyes bulged wide.

The dummy tossed back his head and uttered another cackling laugh. "What's wrong, dude?" he cried. "Slappy got your tongue? Hahahaha!"

Slappy lowered his legs over the counter and kicked the glass with his big shoes. "Hey, whaddaya say?" he shouted. "Let's wish Mister Wood a happy holiday!"

He waved his arms above his head again, and he chanted a stream of strange words . . .

"Amapo Amapi Amapo Golrah Golreeh Amapo!"

A rumbling sound floated through the store. On the floor across from the counter, a stack of Mister Wood cartons began to shake. Slappy repeated the words, waving his wooden hands high. One by one, the boxes popped open.

A Mister Wood dummy rose up from each box. The dummies, with their dimpled smiles, red hair, and freckles, floated from the cartons and landed with their feet on the floor.

Slappy waved his arms some more, and the dummies began to march. Their feet pounded the floor as they stomped their way to the clerk and Mr. Foreman.

"I'm outta here!" the clerk screamed.

He and Mr. Foreman dove for the door. But the army of dummies blocked their way. They raised their arms high and marched around the two men in a tight circle. Faster and faster, until their shoes pounded like thunder on the floor.

"Stop! Let us go!" Mr. Foreman could speak again. He shouted above the din of the marching shoes.

"Hope you guys enjoy your holidays!" Slappy cried. "Knock on wood! Hahaha!"

He dropped to the floor and ran out the door.

"Now let's see what bad deeds I can do for New Year's!"

PART THREE
THE NEXT DAY

What do you think, readers?

Slappy is full of Christmas surprises, isn't he? But *his* surprises don't make you want to say, "Ho ho ho!"

If only Reggie and his family had realized that the dummy was alive when he arrived. He had probably been terrorizing another family somewhere nearby.

Now he's hiding out, planning some New Year's evil. But let me tell you something Slappy doesn't know . . .

The next big surprise will be a bad one for him.

And it's all Darkwell's fault—with the help of Bryce Carlton and his family, that is . . .

Thanks to all of them, this Christmas might be Slappy's last holiday.

Look. Here come Bryce and his dad now, walking down an alley on their way home. Bryce and his family may have a message for Slappy:

"Good-bye forever, Dummy!"

22

When twelve-year-old Bryce Carlton walked anywhere with his dad, Duke Carlton, they looked like big and small versions of the same person. Both Bryce and his dad were built low to the ground and solid.

They both had curly nests of black hair. Big brown raccoon eyes with dark circles around them that gave them a serious expression, even when they weren't being serious.

They were fast talkers and fast walkers. Bryce's teachers were always telling him to slow down:

"Don't run in the halls."

"Take a breath between your sentences."

"What's your hurry?"

Bryce and his dad were happiest when they were outdoors. They loved camping and hiking, and they loved to fish on Tampa Bay from their tiny boat. Bryce even did his homework on the patio behind their house. He hated being cooped up indoors.

Jane Carlton, Bryce's mom, seemed to be from a different family. Her favorite activity was to sit on the couch in their air-conditioned den and read a stack of old novels she brought home from her weekly trips to the library.

She was a research doctor. When she wasn't reading old novels, she spent hours with science and medical journals.

Dr. Carlton was tall and pale and blond. She had a whispery voice and moved quietly. Her footsteps barely made a sound. She was always telling Bryce to use his indoor voice, even when he *was* using his indoor voice!

While Bryce and his dad swam laps in their backyard pool, Bryce's mom worked on her laptop, taking notes or reading new research studies.

Her only outdoor activity was walking Grover, the family dog, around the block a few times a day. Grover had bouncy black curly hair like Bryce and his dad. He was part Lab and part six other dogs. Grover got a lot of Florida sunshine and fresh air because he spent much of his time on a long leash under the family's only tree in the front yard.

A few nights before New Year's, Bryce and his dad were taking a shortcut home after tossing a football around in the park.

It was the end of December, but the Florida air was very warm and humid, and Bryce kept mopping sweat off his forehead with the sleeve of his T-shirt. A pale half-moon floated low in the purple night sky.

They walked down a dark alley that cut through the backs of houses, with kitchen windows sending out patches of orange light. Trash cans were lined up in front of the wooden fences on both sides of the alley.

Two gray cats, their eyes glowing yellow in the dim light, watched the Carltons as they strode by. Somewhere in the distance a car door slammed. Music blared from an open window.

Bryce kicked a stone and watched it bounce across the dirt. His father's sneakers crunched over a long patch of gravel. As they walked, they shuttled the football back and forth to each other.

Bryce stopped suddenly and pointed up ahead. "Dad, what's that?"

Bryce squinted. Sweat blurred his eyes. He mopped it away.

"I think someone's hanging over that garbage can!" Bryce cried.

Yes. The figure slowly came into focus. Someone lay sprawled over the metal can, arms dangling over the sides. Head down, face hidden behind the can.

"Dad—it . . . it's a man!" Bryce stammered. "Is he okay?"

23

"Hey, there—!" Mr. Carlton shouted. He took off running, his sneakers kicking up stones on the dusty alley floor.

Frightened, Bryce held back for a moment. Then he trotted after his dad, eyes on the fallen figure.

"Hey!" Mr. Carlton shouted again. He stopped at the metal can and grabbed for the man's hand.

Bryce stopped a few feet away, his heart pounding. He uttered a startled cry as his dad started to laugh.

Mr. Carlton turned back to Bryce. "Whoa. It's not a man!" he said. "Look. It's some kind of doll."

Bryce stepped up beside his dad. Mr. Carlton grabbed the doll around its suit jacket and hoisted it off the garbage can. The wooden hands hung limply at its sides.

Its glassy green eyes were open wide, as was its red-lipped mouth, painted in a wide grin. The gray suit had some dark stains on one lapel. The doll's red bow tie was crooked and coming untied.

"It's a ventriloquist dummy," Bryce said. "I saw one in an old movie when I was at May-Rose's house."

His dad handed the dummy over to Bryce. It was heavier than Bryce expected. The wooden head tilted to one side. Bryce thought the open-mouthed grin looked kind of eerie.

Bryce held the dummy in one hand and brushed dirt off the front of the suit jacket. "Dad, can I keep him?" he asked. "You know, ever since I saw that one in the movie, I've really wanted one."

Mr. Carlton rubbed dirt off the dummy's shiny black shoe. "Someone must have tossed this dummy in the trash," he said. "Maybe there's something wrong with it."

"I really want it," Bryce said, tilting the head to make it stand up straight. "I think it's awesome, Dad."

"You don't know how long it's been in the garbage, Bryce. It could be full of cockroaches or bedbugs."

"We can take it home and check it," Bryce said. "Please, Dad? Maybe I can do a comedy act with it and surprise May-Rose at her birthday party."

Mr. Carlton took the dummy by the waist and shook it hard. "I don't see any bugs coming off it," he said. He shook it again. The heavy hands banged against the dummy's side.

"I guess it's okay." He handed it back to Bryce.

"Yaaaay!" Bryce let out a cheer and did a happy

dance across the alley, swinging the dummy in front of him.

As he bounced the dummy, a white card slid into view in the dummy's jacket pocket. Bryce pulled out the card and looked at it.

"It says the dummy's name is Slappy, Dad," he said.

Mr. Carlton chuckled. "That's a funny name for a dummy."

"Slappy," Bryce repeated. He slung the dummy over his shoulder and began to walk toward their home. "Slappy and I are going to be best friends!" Bryce exclaimed.

The dummy's grin appeared to grow a little wider.

The next day, Bryce lowered Slappy into his chair at the end of the dinner table. He tucked a clean white napkin under the dummy's chin.

From his new seat at the table, Slappy watched the family. He didn't move, but his mind was working a mile a minute.

My new friend Bryce is an easy victim. Easy-peasy. If I play this right, he'll be my total servant for life. Hahaha.

The new family pleased Slappy. He didn't like pretending to be Mister Wood at Reggie Foreman's house. *Why should someone as brilliant and good-looking as me pretend to be someone else?*

And he didn't like sharing the attention with another dummy in the house, even if Junior was silent and helpless. Slappy laughed to himself. *Hahaha. I ripped him to pieces. He looked better that way!*

Slappy watched the Carltons start to eat their dinner.

Bryce broke off a chunk of bread and dunked it in his lamb stew.

He's a good kid, the dummy thought. *He'll be even better when I teach him who's boss!*

Dr. Carlton looked up from her salad. "Bryce," she said, "does Slappy have to eat *every* meal with us?"

"Of course," Bryce answered. "He's part of the family now, Mom. This is his seat."

"I don't see a problem," Bryce's dad spoke up.

"It's just that Bryce spends all day with that dummy," she said. "Every second. Maybe at dinnertime . . ."

"He likes watching us eat, Mom," Bryce said.

His mom used a silver ladle to drop second helpings of the lamb stew into their soup bowls. "And I suppose you want Slappy to have his own bowl of stew?" she said.

Bryce nodded. "Just give him a small bowl." He pulled out his phone. "I want to take a photo of Slappy eating his stew."

She rolled her eyes. "Isn't this going too far?" she asked Mr. Carlton.

He shrugged. "What's the big deal? If it makes Bryce happy . . ." He chuckled. "It's kind of funny."

"Slappy *is* funny," Bryce said. "I'm making up a lot of good jokes to do with him at May-Rose's birthday party."

"Tell us some of your jokes," his dad said, stirring the stew in his bowl with a spoon.

"No way," Bryce said. "You have to wait till I figure out the whole act with Slappy."

Mr. Carlton lowered his spoon. "Why is Grover barking out there?"

"Someone probably walked by," Bryce said. "He barks every time a stranger passes. He's being a good watchdog."

"Go bring him in. He's been outside all afternoon," Dr. Carlton said. "Maybe Grover would like some stew. If I'm feeding a dummy, I might as well feed the dog, too."

Bryce scooted his chair back and started to the front door. Dr. Carlton waited for the front door to slam behind Bryce. Then she leaned across the table to her husband. "Aren't you a little worried that Bryce has spent every second with this doll?"

He dragged a napkin across his mouth. "Not really," he said. "What's the harm? His friends all went away for the holiday break. Besides, at least he's not playing *Minecraft* twenty hours a day."

The dog came racing in. He went right to his water bowl in the corner and furiously lapped up the whole bowl of water.

"Guess he was thirsty," Bryce said. He dropped back onto his chair and continued to eat the stew.

Dr. Carlton eyed Bryce. "What I don't understand," she said, "is why you put those earbuds in Slappy's ears. Can you explain that?"

"Easy," Bryce said, swallowing a potato. "Sometimes he likes to listen to music."

His mom kept her eyes on Bryce for a long moment, but she didn't reply. Finally, she went back to spooning up her dinner.

A sudden thought flashed through Slappy's mind. It was evening, and he hadn't done his evil deed for the day.

A shiver ran down his back. He had to do something evil today—or he would go to sleep and never wake up.

And who wants to go to sleep when I have a new family to terrify?

"Do you like the stew?" Dr. Carlton asked Bryce. "It's a new recipe."

"I like the meat and potatoes," Bryce said. "But I don't like the carrots. Why do there have to be carrots?"

"It wouldn't be stew if there weren't any carrots," his dad said.

Haha. Ol' Dad is a genius! Slappy thought sarcastically. *Wish I could write that one down. It's a gem!*

As the three Carltons finished their meals, Slappy made a quick move.

He leaned forward and brought his head crashing down. He shattered the bowl and sent lamb stew flying across the table into everyone's laps. Stew oozed over the side and plopped to the floor.

The family cried out, startled. "Slappy fell over!" Bryce yelled.

"He broke the bowl!"

"What a mess."

Mr. Carlton jumped up and began mopping the puddles of stew on the tabletop with his napkin.

Hope they can't see me laughing! Slappy kept his head down. *I'm a baaaad boy!*

He chuckled. *Guess I'll live another day.*

Now . . . what horrible thing can I do to Bryce tomorrow? Hahaha.

Slappy raised his head and glanced at the digital clock on the shelf across from Bryce's bed. 5:03 a.m. The sky outside the bedroom window was still pitch-black.

The house was dark and silent. The only sound Slappy heard was Bryce's soft snores. Slappy sat up at the foot of the bed and listened to the quiet. His mind was spinning with thoughts of the evil deed he had planned the night before.

Nice of Bryce to let me sleep on his bed, Slappy thought. *But why does he have to toss and turn so much? And kick the covers to the floor.*

He disturbed my rest. Slappy shook his head. *I'll have to give him some lessons in keeping still at night. If he doesn't, I'll take over the bed and make him sleep underneath it. Ha! Bryce has some surprises in store.*

Moving silently, Slappy edged himself to the side of the bed and lowered his shoes to the floor. He stretched his arms above his head and bent his knees a few times to get them going.

He didn't mind waking up this early—especially if he could get his evil deed out of the way first thing.

The dummy took his first creeping step. And immediately tripped over something soft on the floor.

Slappy fell to his knees and watched Grover the dog scramble out from under him.

The dog lowered his head and eyed him with a deep growl. Slappy turned to make sure he hadn't awakened Bryce. Asleep on his stomach, his head buried in the pillow, Bryce hadn't moved.

I'll have to teach that mutt a lesson, Slappy thought. *He should know better than to get in my way!*

Grover kept his eyes on the dummy as Slappy tiptoed silently across the room to Bryce's school backpack. Carefully, Slappy reached both hands up and lifted the backpack off the chair.

It was made of canvas, heavier than Slappy thought, filled with textbooks and notebooks. He gave it a hard tug and swung it over his shoulders. Then he turned once again to make sure Bryce was still asleep.

I'm so glad Bryce has a waterproof backpack. This one should hold at least a gallon of water! Hahaha.

Giggling to himself, Slappy entered the hall. *I'm so clever, I wish I could pat myself on the back. I should carry a mirror with me at all times so I can admire myself nonstop.*

The backpack weighed heavily on Slappy's slender shoulders. He leaned forward and pulled himself to the bathroom two doors down.

At the bathroom sink, he giggled again. *Evil is easy,* he told himself. *It's being good that's hard! Hahaha!*

With a groan, he swung the backpack into the sink and unzipped it. He turned on the faucet and watched the backpack fill with cold water.

When the water began to overflow the canvas sides, he shut the faucet and carefully zipped the backpack closed. As he lifted it from the sink, he could feel the water sloshing around inside.

Hee hee. What a hoot! he told himself. *When he gets to school, Bryce will get a D for* drenched*! Of course, everything he owns will be soaked. But it's a small price to pay for having my wonderful company for another day! Haha!*

Slappy lugged the waterlogged backpack to Bryce's bedroom and returned it to the desk chair. Then, stepping around Grover, who had fallen asleep again, the dummy climbed up to his place at the foot of the bed.

The dummy's grin grew wider. *Now I can take the rest of the day off. No need to worry. Evil accomplished!*

As he settled back on top of the covers, Slappy didn't realize that his terrible day had just begun.

When Bryce finally stirred and forced his eyes open, the digital clock read 7:45 a.m. Blinking the sleep from his eyes, he sat up sharply and studied the clock.

"Hey—!" he shouted, loud enough for his parents to hear him downstairs. "Hey—can you hear me? It's almost eight o'clock. Time to get dressed for school. Why didn't anyone wake me up?"

A few seconds later, he heard his mom come to the foot of the stairs. "Bryce, did you forget?" she called. "You're on winter break. There's no school until after New Year's!"

"Oh. Yeah . . . Awesome!" Bryce said. He plopped his head back down on the pillow.

He didn't hear the groan that escaped Slappy's open mouth. *That water gag with the backpack was a waste of time! All that hard work for nothing! He won't even look at his backpack till next week!*

Rolling his eyes, Slappy's brain started spinning. He

had to think of another evil deed for today. If he wanted to live another day, he had to come up with something good . . . good and nasty.

An hour later, Slappy was still thinking hard when Bryce finally pulled himself out of bed and headed for the bathroom.

Evil ideas came naturally to the grinning dummy. *Evil is as evil does,* he told himself. He wasn't sure what that meant, exactly. But he liked it as a slogan for himself.

He remembered how Grover the dog had been in his way and tripped him earlier that morning. *That dog is asking for something horrible to happen to him,* Slappy thought. *Now, don't get me wrong. I'm an animal lover. I love them baked, boiled, or fried! Hahaha!*

Slappy slid down from the bed and made his way to the steps. Dr. Carlton was in the kitchen. He could hear the clatter of silverware and dishes as she began to prepare breakfast.

He climbed silently down the stairs and crept out the front door. It was a sunny, warm Florida morning. Not a cloud in the sky. The air already felt hot and humid.

The dummy stood on the front stoop. He saw Grover halfway down the yard, tied to the shady tree where he usually spent part of his day. He was sitting up, watching two little kids race by on silvery scooters. His tail wagged furiously from side to side.

Bryce really loves his dog. A sick grin spread across Slappy's face. He crept up behind Grover.

Easy-peasy, the dummy told himself. *This is going to be so simple—but so evil.* He rubbed his hands together. *Haha. Sometimes I can't* stand *myself! I'm so awesome and brilliant!"*

So long, Grover. Slappy grabbed the dog's collar to unhook the leash. *Too bad Bryce won't get a chance to say good-bye.*

27

Why do they make these leashes so hard to unfasten?
Slappy grumbled to himself. *Don't they know I have
wooden fingers?*

Grover gazed up at him as he fumbled with the dog's
collar.

Finally, with a loud *click*, the leash snapped open,
and Slappy tossed it across the lawn.

"What are you waiting for?" he shouted at the dog.
"You're free! Free! Get going!"

Grover stared up at him, panting hard, ears perked.

"Run! Go ahead—run! Run like the wind!" Slappy
cried. *"What are you waiting for?"* he asked again.

Grover licked the dummy's hand. His tail wagged
hard, but he didn't move.

Slappy gave the dog a push from behind. *"Don't you
get it, Dog Face? I'm giving you your freedom. You
don't have to thank me. Just run! Run to the next
state!"*

Grover gazed up at him, tail still wagging.

Slappy cried out in frustration. *"Don't just sit there! Move!"* He gave Grover another push. *"Adios! Bon voyage! Happy travels! Go! Send me a postcard when you arrive somewhere!"*

Grover lowered himself on the grass. He tucked his head between his front paws. He yawned.

Slappy groaned. *"Don't you get it, mutt? I just set you free. You can explore the world, see all the sights."*

Grover yawned again. He shut his eyes.

Slappy tried to push him, but he just rolled onto his side. *"Listen to me!"* Slappy cried. *"You've got to do your part. This is where you run away as fast as you can! Listen to me, you . . . you . . ."*

Slappy's voice trailed off. With a sigh, he saw that the dog was fast asleep. He studied Grover. The dog was breathing gently, eyelids fluttering, head resting comfortably on his paws now.

"Strike two," Slappy murmured, shaking his head.

I had a simple plan . . . simply evil. But sometimes even for a genius like me, the simplest plans don't always work out. Well, it's still early, Slappy told himself, glancing at the red morning sun rising over the houses.

And as I always say, the early bird kills the worm. So I'd better get going.

Slappy didn't like failure. And he wanted to be done

with his evil deed so he could relax the rest of the day and dream up even bigger and better horrible deeds for tomorrow.

His head down, lost in thought, he saw something scuttle across the grass behind the sleeping dog. He leaned over to take a closer look. It was a fat brown spider.

"*What a beauty,*" Slappy murmured.

He lifted the spider between two fingers. *Am I lucky or what?* he cackled as he carried it into the house. *My hairy new friend is going to save the day.*

Holding the spider in a tight grip, Slappy crept up to the kitchen doorway. He had to climb into his seat at the table without anyone noticing. He knew his timing had to be perfect.

Dr. Carlton was alone in the kitchen. She stood at the sink, her back turned.

Slappy darted across the room and leaped into his chair at the end of the table. *Ha. She didn't notice.*

Her coffee mug was at her place. He reached across the table and dropped the fat spider into her coffee.

Haha. Wait till she gets a taste of THAT eight-legged beauty! he thought. *She'll totally puke! She'll feel it on her tongue for hours!*

I'm baaaad. I'm really baaad!

Dr. Carlton crossed the room and sat down at her place. She wrapped her hand around the coffee mug and lifted it toward her mouth.

Giggling to himself, Slappy settled back and waited for the fun to begin.

"Good morning." Mr. Carlton entered the kitchen, followed by Bryce.

Dr. Carlton lowered the mug to the table and turned to them. "You two slept pretty late," she said.

Oh, come on! Drink your spider! Slappy urged silently.

Bryce stopped halfway to the table. "Hey, how did Slappy get here?" he asked.

His dad snickered. "You must have brought him down, Bryce. He didn't walk on his own."

Bryce yawned, still half asleep. "Huh? Did I leave him here after dinner last night?"

Stop yakking, Slappy thought. *Let your mother have her little morning surprise!*

He could see the big brown spider bobbing at the top of Dr. Carlton's coffee.

"Bryce, what do you want for breakfast?" she asked.

"Just cereal," Bryce answered. He crossed to the pantry to get a box.

Mr. Carlton poured himself a mug of coffee. He took a long sip.

"Too weak," he said, making a face. "I'm sorry. When I set up the coffee pot last night, I had a feeling the coffee was going to be too weak." He turned to his wife. "Don't drink that. I'll make another pot."

Another pot? Slappy wanted to scream. *No! No other pot! Let her drink what she already has!*

Another evil plan was about to be ruined. That would be strike three for Slappy.

Dr. Carlton slid her coffee mug away from her. "Okay, dear. Make another pot," she said.

Noooooo! Slappy nearly exploded.

But Dr. Carlton raised her mug again. "I'll just take a few sips."

She tilted the mug to her lips and took a few big swallows of coffee.

Yesssss! It was all Slappy could do to keep from bouncing up and down in his seat.

When she returned the mug to the table, the spider was gone.

She rubbed her throat. "Why is your coffee lumpy?" she asked her husband.

Mr. Carlton shrugged. "The next pot will be better."

They didn't see Slappy slump in his chair.

She swallowed it. I can't believe she swallowed the spider.

Strike three! How is this happening? How could that spider fail me?

Bryce sat down and poured himself a bowl of Froot Smacks.

"What are you doing today?" his mother asked. "Do you have any plans?"

"Deshaun is coming over," Bryce said. "He has a new

dirt bike. We're going to take a fast ride to the bay. Hang out for a while."

"Well, you can't hang out too long," Dr. Carlton said, wiping her hands on a dishtowel. "We have a busy day. I want you to help me bake a cake for May-Rose's birthday party tonight."

"Can Deshaun help, too?" Bryce asked.

His mother nodded. "Of course. That would be nice. Does he want to come fishing with us this afternoon? Your dad wants to go out on the water since the weather is so nice."

"Has Deshaun seen Slappy?" Bryce's dad asked.

Bryce poured more cereal into his bowl. "No. I'm going to show him off today."

Dr. Carlton burped.

That's good spider you're burping up! Slappy grumbled.

He wanted to pound his fists on the table. *Three strikes. First the backpack. Then that lazy dog. Now the spider.*

This can't be happening. All my evil tricks are striking out this morning. Easy, Slappy. Calm down, the dummy ordered himself. *You're too awesome—and too evil—to be down for long.*

He knew he had all day to accomplish one evil deed. No need to worry.

And he already had an evil idea that couldn't lose.

He turned to Bryce and watched him crunch down his cereal.

So sorry, my friend, Slappy thought. *But you're going to have a terrible bike accident this morning.*

31

Slappy could always cheer himself up by telling himself how great he was. But there was no time for that this morning. Because of his three failures, he had to focus on his new plan. The words of warning from Darkwell, the sorcerer, were always on his mind.

Doing evil every day was a lot of fun. But he knew it was serious business, too. It was the only way he could stay alive.

Luckily, Bryce carried him outside to wait for Deshaun. And there was Bryce's bike, leaning against the side of the house.

"Bryce, come back in!" his mother called from the front door. "You forgot to brush your teeth."

Bryce set Slappy down on the grass beside the bike and hurried into the house.

Perfect, thought Slappy. *Maybe things are finally going my way.*

He dropped down onto his knees and began to examine the line to the hand brake.

Loosening the brake doesn't take a genius, he thought. *But being one helps! Hahaha.*

After a few minutes, the brake wire jiggled loose in his hand. He pushed it back in place to make it look okay.

Mission accomplished, he told himself. *Bryce may get a few scrapes and bruises. But it will be totally worth it to see him wipe out!*

Slappy was about to climb to his feet when he heard thudding footsteps on the driveway, approaching fast. He turned in time to see Grover leap off the ground, front paws raised, aimed right at the dummy's chest.

Yapping excitedly, the big dog crashed into Slappy.

Ooooof! Slappy fell back with a groan.

The dummy went down on his back, and Grover pounced onto his chest. His tail wagging furiously, the dog nipped and tugged at Slappy's shirt.

"Down! Down! Get off me!" the dummy screeched. *"Go away! You were supposed to run away!"*

Grover didn't seem to understand. Growling excitedly, he bounced on top of the helpless dummy, playfully biting the front of his shirt and jacket.

"Get off! Get off, mutt!" Slappy tried to push the dog off with both hands. But he wasn't strong enough. And Grover was having too much fun to take a hint.

"Go away! You're wrinkling the fabric!" Slappy screamed. He tried rolling out from under the dog. But Grover held on tight and began joyfully licking his face.

"Stop it! Stop!" the dummy begged. "Don't slobber on me! My face is going to warp!"

Finally, the dog toppled off Slappy's chest when he heard footsteps running up the driveway. Slappy raised his head to see Deshaun trotting to the rescue. Deshaun pulled Grover back and lifted the dummy in his other hand.

"Hey—!" Bryce let out a cry as he came bursting out the front door. "How did Grover get loose?"

Deshaun shrugged. "How should I know? I just got here."

Bryce took the dummy from his friend. Grover jumped up, trying to pull Slappy back down. "How did Grover get loose?" Bryce repeated. "What's going on here?"

Deshaun tried to hold Grover down. Grover licked his nose.

Bryce sat Slappy on the lawn and took Grover from Deshaun. He carried the dog to the tree and hooked him back up to the leash.

Slappy stared straight ahead. *That was a close one,* he told himself.

He raised his eyes to the bike. *Happy travels, Bryce, old buddy. Better go easy on the brake. Haha.*

Now I can relax and enjoy myself. My evil work is done for today.

But then, Bryce turned to Deshaun and asked a question—a question that was about to make Slappy's day a whole lot worse.

32

Bryce turned to Deshaun and said, "Hey, where's your bike?"

"It hasn't arrived yet," Deshaun told him. "My dad said it's delayed somewhere. So I brought my skateboard instead."

Bryce sighed. "Bummer. I wanted to see it."

"Me, too," his friend replied. "But do you want to go to the skate park, instead?"

"For sure," Bryce said. He lifted Slappy off the ground. "Let me take this dude up to my room and I'll get my board." He started into the house.

Bryce carried the dummy upstairs and sat him up on his bed.

Slappy's grin remained frozen in place. He gazed blankly across the room.

As Bryce left, he didn't see Slappy's mouth drop open. And he didn't hear his unhappy groan.

Strike four! Slappy told himself. *No bike riding?*

Are you kidding me? This is turning into the worst day ever!

Seminole Sky Drive, Bryce's street, sloped downhill all the way to the park. A few seconds later, Bryce and Deshaun were on their boards, gliding down together.

The air felt fresh and warm against their faces. A car horn honked as they rumbled past, their wheels sending up a roar on the pavement.

"I had this weird dream last night," Bryce said, shouting over the clatter of the skateboards. "Slappy and I were having a snowball fight. Can you believe that? Snow in Tampa?"

Deshaun shook his head. "I've never seen snow," he said. "Except in movies."

"Weird," Bryce said. "You've never left Florida?"

"I've been to South Carolina," Deshaun said. "That's about it."

They stopped for a traffic light. "You dreamed about that doll? What do you do with it?" Deshaun asked.

"He's not a doll," Bryce replied. "He's a ventriloquist dummy. I've been thinking up jokes to do with him. I'm going to take him to my cousin's birthday party tonight and do a comedy act."

"Awesome," Deshaun said.

"He's kind of like a pet. It sounds weird, but sometimes when his eyes are staring at me, I feel like he's alive."

Deshaun snickered. "That's sick. I saw a scary movie on Netflix about an evil dummy that comes alive."

"Slappy isn't evil," Bryce said. "I think he's cute."

The skate park was crowded with kids and teenagers trying out the new boards they got for the holidays.

The park had a 24-foot ledge and a kinked rail. But they headed right to the Ollie Zone to warm up. Bryce wiped out once coming down from a triple ollie. But the only result was a scraped knee, which he considered a win.

They had been there for half an hour when Bryce got a text from his mom: *Cake time. Come home.*

Skating up Seminole Sky Drive was harder than skating down. Bryce turned to Deshaun and shouted over the traffic noise, "Want to come with us this afternoon? We're going fishing on the boat."

"I can't," Deshaun replied. "We have to visit my grandma in St. Pete. But I can stay and help you bake the cake."

"I've got everything ready," Dr. Carlton said when they walked into the kitchen. She pointed to the counter, where large bowls, boxes of ingredients, eggs, butter, and flour were lined up. "Let's get to work.

"Wash your hands and take a seat." She pointed to the three tall stools behind the counter.

"Is it going to be a chocolate cake?" Deshaun asked, after finishing at the sink. He hoisted himself onto the stool at one end. "I'm a chocolate freak."

"Yes, it is. And you can lick the frosting spoon," Dr. Carlton said. "Hey, Bryce—where are you going?"

Bryce was heading to the stairs. "To get Slappy," he said. "He can watch us bake."

"Huh?" His mom squinted at him. "Do we really need that dummy with us for everything we do?"

"Yes," Bryce answered, and disappeared up the stairs.

A minute later, he returned with the grinning dummy in his arms. "Now we can start," Bryce said. He sat Slappy down carefully on the stool at the other end of the counter.

Slappy eyed the glass mixing bowls and all the ingredients. He wanted to rub his hands together gleefully.

I'm ready, he thought. *Ready to cook up something awful. Haha. Look out, world. My luck is about to change!*

33

Bryce climbed up on his knees on the stool between Deshaun and Slappy. "What do we do first?" he asked.

Dr. Carlton slid the egg carton across the counter. "I've already beaten the butter and sugar together. Now you'll crack four eggs and drop them into the big mixing bowl," she instructed.

Bryce cracked an egg against the side of the bowl. The shell crumpled in his hand and the egg oozed into the bowl. Deshaun cracked one next. Then one more egg each, and they were ready for the flour.

"Measure out three cups," his mother said, handing Bryce the bag.

Both boys perched on their knees, side by side on the tall stools, following Dr. Carlton's directions. It didn't take long to get all the cake ingredients into the large glass bowl.

"Here is the magical part," Dr. Carlton said, handing Bryce a long-handled wooden spoon. "Start stirring, and in a very short while, it will turn into chocolate cake batter."

Bryce took the spoon and leaned over the bowl. "It's real gooey," he said as he began to stir.

"It will thicken up as you stir it," his mom said.

"It's very chocolatey, too," Deshaun said.

"Stir a little harder. Scoop the batter up from the bottom," Dr. Carlton told Bryce as the phone rang. "Be right back." She hurried from the room.

Bryce leaned over the bowl and stirred harder.

Showtime! thought Slappy. He waited till Deshaun had turned his gaze to the window. Then he raised his wooden hands—and gave Bryce a hard shove from behind.

"Hey—!" Bryce toppled forward. His head went down and plunged into the thick, chocolatey batter.

Oh, too bad! Slappy told himself. *Bryce just ruined the cake. Hahaha. He's in major trouble now. Now I'm really a baaaaad boy!*

Bryce came up sputtering and choking. He used both hands to wipe the gooey globs of batter from his eyes and nose. He frantically mopped his face with his shirt sleeve, trying to get it all off before his mom returned.

Batter covered his hair and oozed down his forehead. "Deshaun!" he screamed. "Why did you push me?"

Deshaun gasped. "Huh? Push you? No way, dude!"

"You—you shoved me!" Bryce yelled, spitting chocolatey batter from his mouth.

Slappy giggled to himself. *This is working out better than I thought! Not only did Bryce ruin the cake, he's going to ruin his friendship, too! Haha.*

"You fell into the bowl!" Deshaun cried. "Now you're trying to blame *me*?"

"What's all the screaming?" Dr. Carlton came running back into the kitchen.

Poor Bryce, Slappy thought. *He's in deep trouble now. He'll probably be grounded for life!*

Slappy froze, waiting for Bryce's mom to explode in anger. But to his surprise, she burst out laughing. She stared at Bryce, his head covered in gloppy cake batter, and laughed till tears ran from her eyes.

"You look so hilarious!" she cried. "Like a monster from a horror movie!"

Deshaun laughed, too. *"The Monster from the Cake Bowl!"* he cried.

Bryce wiped at his hair.

"No! Don't move!" Dr. Carlton said. "Don't wipe it off. I have to take a photo!"

She rushed from the room and came back a few seconds later with her phone. "Stay right there, Bryce." She began snapping photos. "We'll use one of these as a birthday card for May-Rose. And we'll stop and buy a cake for her on the way to her house. This is going to be perfect."

Whoa. Hold your horses! Slappy groaned. *This is not the way it's supposed to go!*

He watched the three of them laughing and having a good time.

Am I slipping? Is the great Slappy losing his touch? the dummy asked himself. *What's wrong with these people? They shouldn't be laughing. They should be* screaming!

He snapped his eyes shut. *I've got to work harder. This day is going to ruin my brilliant reputation. Uh-oh. Forget my reputation! This could be my last day alive on earth!*

Deshaun went home. Bryce and his mom cleaned up the kitchen. Then Bryce took a shower to wash off the chocolate batter.

Slappy sat on the tall kitchen stool, thinking hard. He could feel waves of heavy panic rolling up and down his body.

I make other people panic! he thought. *How can this be happening to me?*

How can I be so close to going to sleep forever?

He needed the perfect idea. Something simple but evil. Something that couldn't go wrong.

A short while later, Dr. Carlton came into the kitchen. She began pulling food from the fridge. Slappy watched her making a stack of sandwiches to take on the afternoon fishing trip.

Humming to herself, she wrapped each sandwich. Then she stuffed them all into a big blue cooler.

As she headed upstairs to change, the kitchen door opened, and Mr. Carlton walked in, carrying two white cartons, one in each hand. Bait for the family fishing trip.

"I've got the worms!" he shouted up to her. "We're all set to go!" He set the cartons on the counter beside the kitchen sink.

Haha! I'm set to go, too! Slappy laughed.

Suddenly, he had the best idea ever!

Slappy waited till the kitchen was empty. Then he slid down off the tall stool and made his way to the sink.

He hoisted himself up onto the counter and opened the blue cooler.

These sandwiches look tasty, he thought. *But I can make them even tastier!*

Slappy could hear voices in the living room. He had to work fast.

He quickly unwrapped the sandwiches. *Yum. Egg salad. Tuna salad. Ham and cheese.*

Then he opened a carton of worms and dumped them into the sandwiches.

Quickly wrapping everything up, Slappy laughed. *Haha. I'm so evil, it HURTS! Worm salad sandwiches for everyone! I can't wait till lunchtime! Hahaha!*

"Is everyone ready?" Mr. Carlton backed into the kitchen carrying two fishing poles. "Do you have caps to wear? The sun gets pretty strong out on the water."

Bryce walked in and saw Slappy sitting on the counter by the sink. "Weird," he said. "Why did you move Slappy from the stool?"

"I didn't move him," his dad answered.

"Maybe Mom did." Bryce picked the dummy up. "Can Slappy come fishing with us?"

His dad chuckled. "I guess. If we run into any really big fish, we can use him for bait!"

"Not funny, Dad," Bryce said. "Slappy is my pal."

Mr. Carlton shook his head and tsk-tsked. "You and that dummy . . ."

Bryce tucked Slappy under his arm. Dr. Carlton followed them out to the SUV, adjusting a Tampa Bay Rays baseball cap over her hair. "Beautiful day to be out on the water," she said. "Hard to believe it's the end of December."

The drive to the pier at the bay took nearly an hour. Slappy sat beside Bryce in the backseat, his grin even wider than usual. He couldn't wait for the Carltons to open their cooler. *Lunch is going to be a SCREAM!*

"Slappy's first fishing trip," Bryce said. "This is awesome."

"I hope he doesn't get seasick," Mr. Carlton joked.

"Are you bringing him to May-Rose's party tonight?" his mother asked.

"Yes. I worked up some jokes to perform for her."

Mr. Carlton parked their SUV across from the dock.

Their little white boat bobbed in the gentle bay water. The breeze off the bay felt warm. Seagulls squawked somewhere in the distance.

Bryce climbed out from the backseat and followed his dad to the rear of the car, carrying Slappy with him. Mr. Carlton opened the trunk and began to pull out the fishing poles.

But he stopped suddenly and left the poles lying where they were. "Oh no!" he cried. He slapped his forehead and turned to Bryce. "Would you believe it? I forgot to bring the sandwiches! I left the cooler in the kitchen!"

36

No one saw Slappy roll his eyes and gnash his teeth.
No! No! Nooooo! This isn't happening! he wailed to
himself. *I've never had a horrible day like this! I'm not
ready to say, "Good-bye, World!" I'm too wonderful to
go out like this!*

"There's a deli down the road," Dr. Carlton said.
"Let's buy some sandwiches instead."

Mr. Carlton closed the back of the SUV. He shook his
head. "How could I be so forgetful?"

Yes. How COULD you? Slappy thought. *How could
you do this to me?*

Slappy didn't have a heart. But he could feel a fluttering in his chest. He knew it was total terror. *I need
to stay alive,* he thought. *What a sad place this world
would be without ME!*

Bryce and his parents headed down the dock. "Bryce,
put the dummy down," his dad said. "Leave him here.

You don't need to carry him all the way to the store and back."

Bryce sat Slappy down on the edge of the wooden pier. Someone had left a gray metal toolbox there, and Bryce leaned Slappy against it. Then he followed his parents down the narrow dirt road.

Thinking hard, Slappy watched their little boat bobbing at the side of the dock. *I know what my problem is today,* he told himself. *I haven't been evil enough.*

"No more Mister Nice Guy!" he cried aloud.

He climbed to his feet. Then he bent down and opened the toolbox. "What have we got here? A nice-looking drill!" He cackled as he lifted it from the box.

I know what their boat could use, he thought, spinning the drill in his hands. *I'm going to decorate it with a few holes in the bottom! Haha!*

Slappy walked to the side of the dock. He lowered himself to his knees. Then he reached down into the boat and began to drill.

He cackled again. *They won't notice till the boat is halfway out and starts to sink. Then they'll enjoy a nice swim back to shore!*

Slappy drilled two small holes in the bottom of the boat and started a third. *"This can't fail!"* he shouted out loud. *"Another day, another brilliant bit of evil! Slappy lives!"*

Slappy returned the drill to the toolbox and dropped back onto the dock just as Bryce and his parents returned.

Enjoy the water, everyone! Slappy thought. He wanted to burst out laughing.

Slappy saves the day—for Slappy!

"Want me to put the bag of sandwiches on the boat?" Bryce asked.

Mr. Carlton shook his head. A grin spread across his face. "I have a surprise for you two," he said.

Slappy's eyes popped wide. *Huh? A surprise?*

"We're not taking our creaky little boat," Bryce's dad announced. "My friend Andrew is picking us up in his power cruiser. We're fishing in style today!"

Bryce pointed out to the water. "Hey, here he comes now. Wow! Check out that awesome boat!"

No! No! No! Their eyes were on the gleaming white boat roaring toward them. No one saw Slappy bang his head with both fists. *Now what? Everything I try goes haywire.* He slapped his head again. *Think, Slappy! Think!*

Bryce carried Slappy onto the deck and sat him down on the bench beside him. The boat rocked, as if eager to get going.

What an awesome day! Bryce thought.

What a nightmarish day! Slappy thought.

The boat jolted hard as the motor roared to life and zoomed away from the dock. Bryce was rocked forward and nearly fell off the bench.

Yes! An idea! Slappy silently exclaimed. *I can save myself. This idea can't fail!*

37

I'll push Bryce overboard, Slappy decided.

The water is pretty shallow here, and he's a good swimmer.

It will just spoil his day.

But it will MAKE mine! Hahaha.

The motor roared as the boat powered farther out into the sparkling bay. The waves splashed against the sides. The wind swirled around them, fresh and cool.

Now's my chance! Slappy grinned, as Bryce leaned over the side, gazing into the rippling water.

Perfect, Slappy thought. *Don't move.*

He crept over to Bryce. He raised both hands behind Bryce's back.

And then Slappy shoved hard.

And just as he did, the boat hit a strong current— and it bounced up over the water.

Slappy uttered a silent scream as he lurched off the deck—and sailed headfirst into the bay.

"Help! Oh noooo!! Slappy fell overboard!" Bryce shouted. "Help!"

Thrashing and kicking in the bouncing water, Slappy felt panic sweep over him. *I can't swim! I can't swim!*

He sank beneath the surface, then bobbed up again. The strong current was carrying him away from the boat.

I'm too brilliant to drown! Isn't anyone going to rescue me?

He heard a splash. And then the sounds of someone swimming toward him, taking long strokes, kicking furiously.

Bryce!

Swimming hard, Bryce wrapped his arm under one of Slappy's and swam back to the boat with him.

Mr. Carlton helped Bryce and the dummy back into the boat. "He's soaked through and through," he told Bryce. He shook his head. "Totally waterlogged. I'm not sure if he'll ever be the same."

"M-maybe we can dry him out," Bryce stammered.

Water dripped off Slappy and splashed onto the deck. *I KNOW I'll never be the same,* Slappy thought.

As soon as they returned home, Mr. Carlton and

Bryce took the soaked dummy upstairs. Mr. Carlton draped him over the bathtub. "Give him a few days," he told Bryce. "Maybe he'll dry out."

A few days? Slappy shook his head. *I don't have a few days. I only have a few HOURS!*

"Better get changed for May-Rose's party," Slappy heard Mr. Carlton tell Bryce out in the hall.

The birthday party!

Slappy raised his head. *Yes! Yes! I'm excellent at birthday parties,* he told himself. *Birthday parties are my SPECIALTY!*

Memories flashed through his mind. Slappy remembered other birthday parties he had ruined. And it gave him hope. *The day is almost over. But I still have one last chance.*

He began to plan what he would do at May-Rose's party.

I can smash the birthday cake. Then I can rip apart all the presents. I'm a real party animal. I can pinch the kids. Or I can bite them! I can make all the guests cry. Haha!

Giggling to himself, he remembered one of his favorite birthday parties. He spewed hot, disgusting green slime on all the guests. They all screamed in horror and ran out of the house wailing and puking.

One of my best performances ever . . .

Slappy knew he could do it again. Yes, it had been a terrible day. But he had one more chance.

His painted grin grew wider. *"There's no way I can fail at a birthday party!"*

A short while later, Slappy heard Mr. Carlton climb the stairs. "Bryce, are you ready?" he called.

Bryce stepped out of his room. "Is this T-shirt okay?" he asked.

"Is it clean?" his dad asked. "Yes. It's fine. Let's go. We're a little late."

Slappy heard the two of them head for the stairs.

Hey—you're forgetting someone! he thought. *Don't forget ME!*

Then he heard Bryce stop. "We're forgetting Slappy," Bryce said. "I practiced a comedy act with him to perform for May-Rose."

Thank goodness! Slappy exclaimed to himself.

But then, Mr. Carlton's words chilled the dummy. "No way, Bryce. That dummy is still soaked through and through. I don't want him in my car."

"But, Dad—"

"No. Sorry. Slappy has to stay home," Mr. Carlton insisted. "You can't bring him."

A long moment of silence. Finally Slappy heard

Bryce say, "Okay, Dad. Let's go." Then the two of them hurried down the stairs.

Each footstep sounded like a drumbeat to Slappy. A funeral drumbeat. He stared down into the bathtub, shaking his head.

"This is it. It's over. I'm doomed," he murmured. *"I'm one dead dummy!"*

PART FOUR
LATER THAT NIGHT

Well, readers, you'll have to admit it's looking pretty bad for Slappy.

The day has gone from bad—to worse—to *horribly worse* for the evil dummy.

Seems this is his last night alive on earth.

Do you want to send him a good-bye note?

I may tell you how at the end of the book . . .

Slappy lifted himself off the side of the bathtub and sat down in a wet heap on the floor. He bowed his head and shut his eyes. He heard the front door close downstairs and knew he was alone.

Wait. Is this it? Is it over for me? No way! A genius like me never says die! he told himself.

Yes, today is almost over. And my evil has failed every time. But I'm too awesome to give up!

There are a few hours left. I still have a chance!

Tugging down the sleeves of his wet suit jacket, he climbed to his feet. His shoes made a *squish squish* sound as he stepped out of the bathroom.

"*I'll walk to the birthday party.*" Slappy squished his way down the stairs, leaving puddles of water in his path. He made his way to the front door and stepped outside.

The air felt cool and damp. He shivered and started

down the driveway. A burst of wind pushed him back. It swirled around him and howled in his ears.

Water dripped down the sides of his face. Slappy fumbled in the wet pockets of his jacket. He tugged out the earbuds Bryce had given him. He tucked them into his ears to keep the water out.

I need to concentrate on my evil.

He crossed his arms, lowered his head, and leaned into the wind. As the gusting wind pushed against him, he staggered toward May-Rose's house six blocks away.

"*Oh!*" A puff of black smoke exploded in front of him, and he stopped short with a startled cry. The earbuds fell from his ears.

As he stooped to pick them up, the black smoke cleared. And a figure stepped out of the shadows.

"*Father!*" Slappy cried. "*I . . . I don't believe it's you!*"

Yes, standing in front of the dummy in his black robe and hood was the sorcerer, Darkwell.

"*Father!*" Slappy repeated. "*What are you doing here? What do you want?*"

The old sorcerer swept his robe around himself and narrowed his eyes at Slappy. "I've come to destroy you," he boomed. "Your days of evildoing are over!"

The shock of Darkwell's words made Slappy drop to his knees. *"But, Father!"* he cried. *"You created me to be evil. You forced me to do an evil deed a day to stay alive."*

Darkwell frowned and shook his head. "That wasn't true," he said in a gruff whisper. "I'm afraid I lied to you, Slappy. I made up that story about having to be evil every day."

"But—but . . . why?" Slappy stammered.

"I wanted to take revenge upon the world," the old sorcerer replied. "And that was my way to make sure you'd do what I asked!"

"You mean I didn't have to be evil every day?" Slappy demanded.

Darkwell nodded. "No. You didn't. I never cast a spell like that on you. It was all a lie."

"B-but, Father—" Slappy sputtered. *"I enjoy being evil! And I'm so good at it!"*

"No more!" Darkwell boomed. He raised both hands above his head. "Things have changed. I've changed. I have made my peace with the world. I have decided to do only *good* from now on."

"Don't you want to think this over?" Slappy asked.

"My first good deed," Darkwell replied, "will be to rid the world of you and your evil."

Slappy's legs trembled as he climbed to his feet to plead with the sorcerer. *"Maybe you could cut me some slack? Umm ... Maybe I could just do evil on Tuesdays and Thursdays?"*

"Enough!" Darkwell cried, his voice booming against the howling wind. "When I say the secret words in reverse, you will go to sleep, Slappy. And you will sleep forever." He took a deep breath. "Good-bye, my son!"

"No! I don't want to hear it!" Slappy wailed. He jammed the earbuds back into his ears. *"No! You can't do this! Don't hurt me, Father. Don't put me to sleep."*

Slappy rushed forward. But Darkwell shoved him away. And then the sorcerer called out the secret words in reverse:

"Karrano Molonu Loma Odonna Marri Karru!"

A low groan, long and sad, rose up from deep inside the dummy. Slappy's eyes closed. His legs fell limp, and he slumped facedown onto the grass.

He didn't move.

The wind swirled harder, howling through the trees.

Clouds floated over the moon, sending heavy black shadows over the grass.

Darkwell stood over the fallen dummy for a long moment, silent and still. He held his breath. He stared, unblinking. He stood watching until he was satisfied that Slappy was no longer alive.

Then he vanished in another puff of black smoke.

THE END

. . .

OR IS IT?

EPILOGUE

The wind howled, shaking the trees. The grass bent in waves under the bursts of air.

The dummy didn't move. He lay facedown with his arms spread above his head, as if reaching across the lawn.

Put to sleep. Put to sleep forever, by the sorcerer who had created him.

Was it true?

No more evil dummy.

No more Slappy.

No.

It wasn't true.

Slappy raised his head from the ground. He opened his eyes and blinked a few times. Shaking his head as if shaking himself awake, he sat up.

He gazed at the shadowy lawns. There was no one in sight.

He stretched both arms above his head. Then he lowered his hands and pulled the earbuds from his ears.

Haha! His plan had worked!

You don't know everything, Father! The spell doesn't work if I can't hear it!

Slappy chuckled. *"Darkwell never was a very good sorcerer!"*

The dummy tossed the earbuds across the grass. Then he climbed to his feet.

"Now," he said, *"let's get to May-Rose's house and have some fun! Hahahaha!"*

REALLY THE END

Turn the page—if you dare—and take
a deep dive into the twisted mind of

SLAPPY!

TABLE OF CONTENTS

SLAPPY'S MOST ICONIC INSULTS

Slappy here, everyone. I know you're glad to see me. I heard your screams. But try to control your overwhelming love for me as you bask in my greatness. I'm a poet . . . and I know it! Here are some of my best lines ever! Haha!

Slappy on . . . You

You need a checkup from the neck up.

Is that your face, or did you forget to take out the garbage?

Is that your face, or are you standing on your head?

The only thing your head is good for is to keep your hat off your shoulders!

I like your long hair. Too bad it's all growing on your back!

Where did you two meet? A nerd circus?

Slappy on . . . Dummies

How about a game of Kick the Dummy Down the Stairs? We'll take turns being the dummy. You can go first!

You're so dumb, you stay up all night studying how to pick your nose!

You're so stupid, you have to study up before you can BURP!

You failed your IQ test because you couldn't spell IQ.

Of course you feel light-headed. There's no brain in there!

Your brain is impossible! Impossible to FIND!

Slappy on . . . Himself

Everyone loves Slappy. Even the termites inside my head think I'm delicious!

I would call myself an awesome genius. But, you know, someone as brilliant and perfect as I am doesn't like to brag.

I was a real star in kindergarten. That's because all the others in my class were *dummies*!

My IQ is so high, I need a ladder to read it!

I'm so brilliant, I'm the only one who can outsmart myself!

I'm so bright, I use my own head as a night-light!

I'm so smart, the dictionary asked me to define it.

I'm so awesome, I want to turn my mouth

around and kiss myself! (But I don't want to get splinters!)

JOKE'S ON YOU

There's no one funnier than me. NO ONE. If you don't laugh, I'll bite you!

Slappy: Knock, knock
Human: Who's there?
Slappy: Jane
Human: Jane who?
Slappy: Jane jer clothes. You stink!

Do you know the best thing about being a jack-in-the-box? It's always *spring*time!

Know why I was the smartest one in my class? Because I was the only one in my class!

Slappy: Know what would help you be smarter?
Human: No.
Slappy: I don't know, either!

What did the doctor say when the Invisible Man came to his office?
Sorry, I can't see you now.

Know why I get invited to so many parties?
Because I'm a SCREAM!

INTERVIEW WITH A DUMMY

My Interview with Slappy

By R.L. Stine

SLAPPY: Before you start asking me questions, R.L., I have a question for *you*. Why do you enjoy writing about me so much? Is it because I'm brilliant and clever and wise? Or is it because I'm so good-looking? Did you know when I look in a mirror, the mirror says, "Thank you!"

R.L.: I like to write about you because you're so modest, Slappy.

SLAPPY: When *you* look in a mirror, the

mirror says, "Humans Only!" Hahaha.

R.L.: And you're always so kind.

SLAPPY: I'm kind to animals. I never step on them unless they're in my way!

R.L.: Let me ask you this: Do you have a personal motto?

SLAPPY: I'm a big believer in the Golden Rule. "Do it to others before they do it to you!" Hahaha.

R.L.: That's kind of evil.

SLAPPY: Your *face* is kind of evil. Does it hurt you?

R.L.: No.

SLAPPY: Well, it's *killing* me! Hahaha!

R.L.: A lot of people want to know what's your favorite food.

SLAPPY: Well, fifth graders are my favorite. But sixth graders can be delicious, too. They're a little tough, so you have to cook them longer. Haha.

R.L.: Do you have any heroes? Anyone you truly admire?

SLAPPY: Yes, *I'm* my biggest hero. I'm not very tall, but I really look up to myself! Haha. If I could be like anyone, I'd be just like me. I'm so great, people burst into applause every time I leave a room!

R.L.: What do you admire most about yourself?

SLAPPY: Shall I make a list for you? There are so many things to admire. I would never brag. So I just come out and admit that I'm perfect in every way.

R.L.: What's a hidden talent of yours that no one knows about?

SLAPPY: I'm an awesome jazz piano player.

R.L.: Huh? I'm amazed. I never knew that.

SLAPPY: My other hidden talent is that I'm an awesome LIAR. Hahaha.

R.L.: How did you get so evil?

SLAPPY: I took a course online.

R.L.: If you could travel in time to any point in history, where would you go?

SLAPPY: I'd go back to this morning before you showed up! Haha.

R.L.: What's the most evil thing you did today?

SLAPPY: Well, I left the cap off the toothpaste this morning. I can't help it. I'm just a BAAAD BOY!

R.L.: Slappy, what advice would you give other dummies?

SLAPPY: Don't call me dummy, dummy!

R.L.: One last question. What gives you goosebumps?

SLAPPY: Nothing gives me more goose-bumps than doing my job. What's my job? Scaring kids, of course! It's a dangerous job, but some-one has to do it. Luckily, I have a knack for it. Remember, there are no bad kids in the world— only kids screaming in terror! Haha. Hey, I'm giving *myself* goosebumps!

Catch the
MOST WANTED
Goosebumps® villains
UNDEAD OR ALIVE!

SPECIAL EDITIONS

THE SCARIEST PLACE ON EARTH!

HELP! WE HAVE STRANGE POWERS!
R.L. STINE

ESCAPE FROM HORRORLAND
R.L. STINE

THE STREETS OF PANIC PARK
R.L. STINE

WHEN THE GHOST DOG HOWLS
R.L. STINE

LITTLE SHOP OF HAMSTERS
R.L. STINE

HEADS, YOU LOSE!
R.L. STINE

WEIRDO HALLOWEEN
R.L. STINE

THE WIZARD OF OOZE
R.L. STINE

SLAPPY NEW YEAR!
R.L. STINE

THE HORROR AT CHILLER HOUSE
R.L. STINE

HALL OF HORRORS—HALL OF FAME
FOR THE TRULY TERRIFYING!

CLAWS!
R.L. STINE

NIGHT OF THE GIANT EVERYTHING
R.L. STINE

SCHOLASTIC

www.scholastic.com/goosebumps

GBHL19H2

The Original Bone-Chilling Series

—with Exclusive
Author Interviews!

NIGHT of the LIVING DUMMY
R.L. STINE

DEEP TROUBLE
R.L. STINE

MONSTER BLOOD
R.L. STINE

The HAUNTED MASK
R.L. STINE

ONE DAY at HORRORLAND
R.L. STINE

the CURSE of the MUMMY'S TOMB
R.L. STINE

BE CAREFUL WHAT YOU WISH FOR
R.L. STINE

SAY CHEESE and DIE!
R.L. STINE

the HORROR at CAMP JELLYJAM
R.L. STINE

HOW I GOT MY SHRUNKEN HEAD
R.L. STINE

R. L. Stine's Fright Fest!

Now with Splat Stats and More!

GET YOUR HANDS ON THEM B[EFORE]
THEY GET THEIR HANDS ON Y[OU]

ALL 62 ORIGINAL
Goosebumps
AVAILABLE
IN EBOOK!

SCHOLASTIC
scholastic.com

GBCLRP2

CONTINUE THE FRIGHT AT THE GOOSEBUMPS SITE

scholastic.com/goosebumps

FANS OF GOOSEBUMPS CAN:

- PLAY THE GHOULISH GAME:
  GOOSEBUMPS: SLAPPY'S DROP DEAD HOUSE

- LEARN ABOUT NEW BOOKS AND TERRIFYING CLASSICS

- TAKE A QUIZ AND LEARN WHICH TYPE OF MONSTER YOU ARE!

- LEARN ABOUT THE AUTHOR WHO STARTED IT ALL: R.L. STINE

■ SCHOLASTIC

GBWEB2019

THE Goosebumps SERIES COMES TO LIFE
IN A BRAND-NEW DIGITAL WORLD

MEET Slappy—and explore the Goosebumps Zone.
PLAY games, create an avatar, and chat with other fans.

Start your
adventure today!
Download the
HOME BASE app
and scan this
image to unlock
exclusive rewards!

SCHOLASTIC.COM/HOMEBASE

SCHOLASTIC

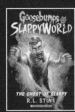

ALWAYS SLAPPY TO SEE YOU!

Goosebumps MOST WANTED
SON OF SLAPPY
R.L. STINE

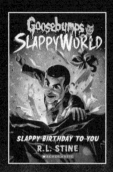

Goosebumps SLAPPYWORLD
SLAPPY BIRTHDAY TO YOU
R.L. STINE

Goosebumps SLAPPYWORLD
I AM SLAPPY'S EVIL TWIN
R.L. STINE

Goosebumps SLAPPYWORLD
THE GHOST OF SLAPPY
R.L. STINE

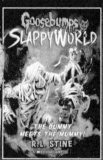

Goosebumps SLAPPYWORLD
THE DUMMY MEETS THE MUMMY!
R.L. STINE

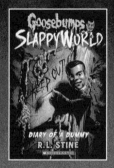

Goosebumps SLAPPYWORLD
DIARY OF A DUMMY
R.L. STINE

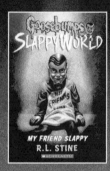

Goosebumps SLAPPYWORLD
MY FRIEND SLAPPY
R.L. STINE

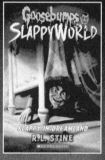

Goosebumps SLAPPYWORLD
SLAPPY IN DREAMLAND
R.L. STINE

Goosebumps
NIGHT of the LIVING DUMMY
R.L. STINE

Goosebumps
NIGHT of the LIVING DUMMY 2
R.L. STINE

Goosebumps
NIGHT of the LIVING DUMMY 3
R.L. STINE

Goosebumps
BRIDE of the LIVING DUMMY
R.L. STINE

COLLECT ALL OF SLAPPY'S TERRIFYING TALES!

SCHOLASTIC

SLAPPY-BEWARE

About the Author

R.L. Stine says he gets to scare people all over the world. So far, his books have sold more than 400 million copies, making him one of the most popular children's authors in history. The Goosebumps series has more than 150 titles and has inspired a TV series and two motion pictures. R.L. himself is a character in the movies! He has also written the teen series Fear Street, and the Mostly Ghostly and Nightmare Room series. He is currently writing a series of graphic novels entitled Just Beyond. R.L. Stine lives in New York City with his wife, Jane, an editor and publisher. You can learn more about him at rlstine.com.